Will, Climb to

BETWEEN HEAVEN AND EARTH!

ERIC WALTERS

BETWEEN HEAVEN AND EARTH

ORCA BOOK PUBLISHERS

Library and Archives Canada Cataloguing in Publication

Walters, Eric, 1957-
Between heaven and earth / Eric Walters.
(Seven (the series))

Issued also in an electronic format.
ISBN 978-1-55469-941-4

I. Title. II. Series: Seven the series
PS8595.A598B47 2012 jc813'.54 C2012-902584-4

First published in the United States, 2012
Library of Congress Control Number: 2012938222

Summary: DJ climbs Mount Kilimanjaro to scatter his beloved grandfather's ashes.

Orca Book Publishers is dedicated to preserving the environment and has printed this book on Forest Stewardship Council® certified paper.

Orca Book Publishers gratefully acknowledges the support for its publishing programs provided by the following agencies: the Government of Canada through the Canada Book Fund and the Canada Council for the Arts, and the Province of British Columbia through the BC Arts Council and the Book Publishing Tax Credit.

Design by Teresa Bubela
Cover photography by Getty Images

ORCA BOOK PUBLISHERS
PO Box 5626, Stn. B
Victoria, BC Canada
V8R 6S4

ORCA BOOK PUBLISHERS
PO Box 468
Custer, WA USA
98240-0468

www.orcabook.com
Printed and bound in Canada.

16 15 14 13 • 7 6 5 4

For Nick Mednis, my kind, gentle father-in-law. He was a wonderful father and grandfather. All the grandchildren called him "Tampa" because the first to come along couldn't pronounce Grandpa. *He almost always had a smile on his face and often a simple beret on his head as he walked. The beret I gave the grandfather in this story was to honor my children's Tampa. I took it with me when my son and I climbed Kilimanjaro. I think that would have made Tampa smile.*

R.I.P. greatest Grandpa EVER!

David McLean

Ann

Deborah

← our moms and aunts →

twins

DJ

Steve

bros

Spencer

everyone calls him Bunny

~~Bernard~~

the youngest at 15

ERIC WALTERS
BETWEEN HEAVEN AND EARTH

JOHN WILSON
LOST CAUSE

TED STAUNTON
JUMP CUT

RICHARD SCRIMGER
INK ME

climbing Mt. Kilimanjaro

Actually going to make it to Spain this summer!

making movies in Buffalo

LOOSE in downtown Toronto

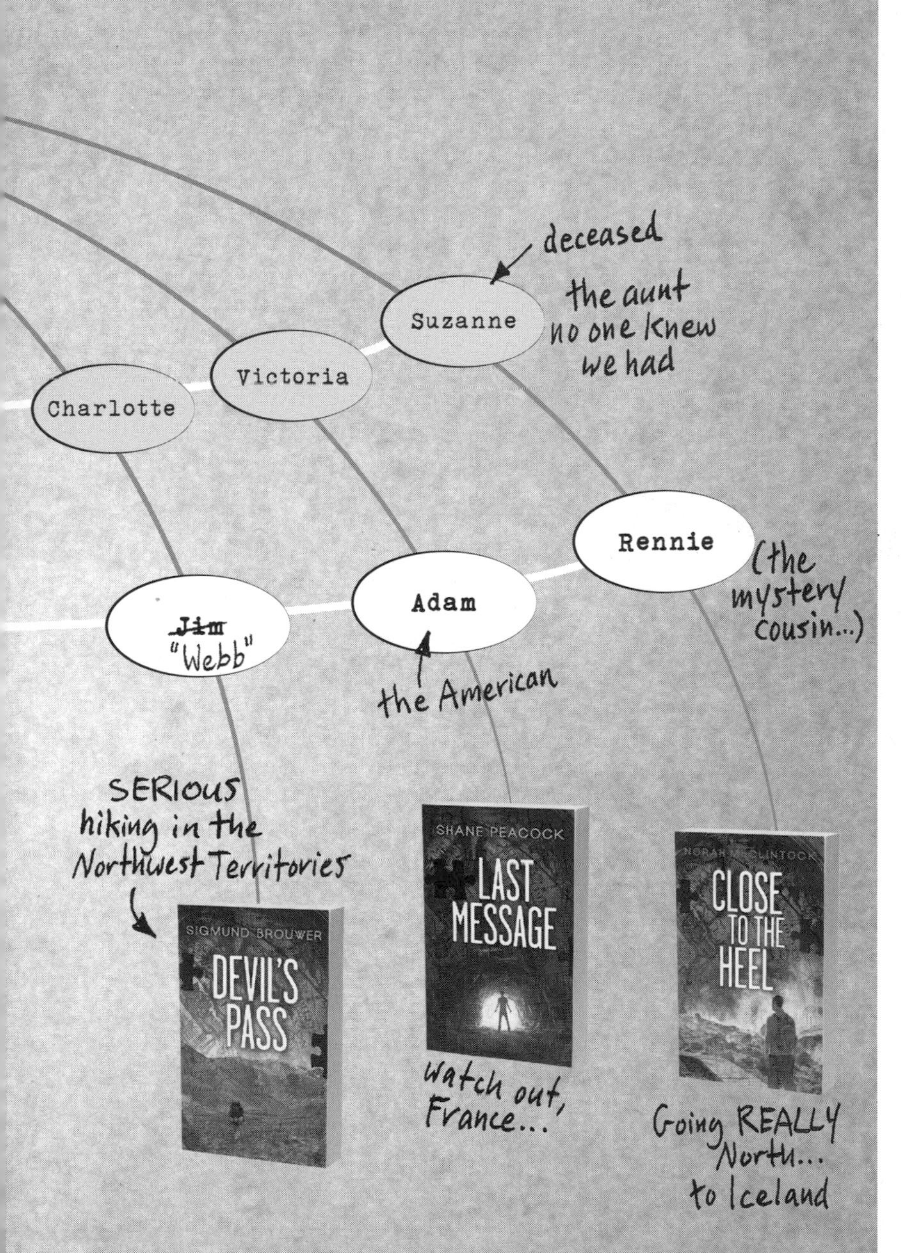
deceased
Suzanne
the aunt no one knew we had
Victoria
Charlotte
Rennie
(the mystery cousin...)
Adam
Jim "Webb"
the American
SERIOUS hiking in the Northwest Territories
SIGMUND BROUWER
DEVIL'S PASS
SHANE PEACOCK
LAST MESSAGE
Watch out, France...!
NORAH McCLINTOCK
CLOSE TO THE HEEL
Going REALLY North... to Iceland

Arctic Ocean
CANADA
NORTH
AMERICA
UNITED STATES
Spencer
Toronto
Bunny
Buffalo
Webb
Pacific
Ocean
KENYA
RWANDA
BURUNDI
Mount
Kilimanjaro
Moshi
DEMOCRATIC
REPUBLIC
OF THE CONGO
Dar es Salaam
TANZANIA
ZAMBIA
MALAWI
MOZAMBIQUE

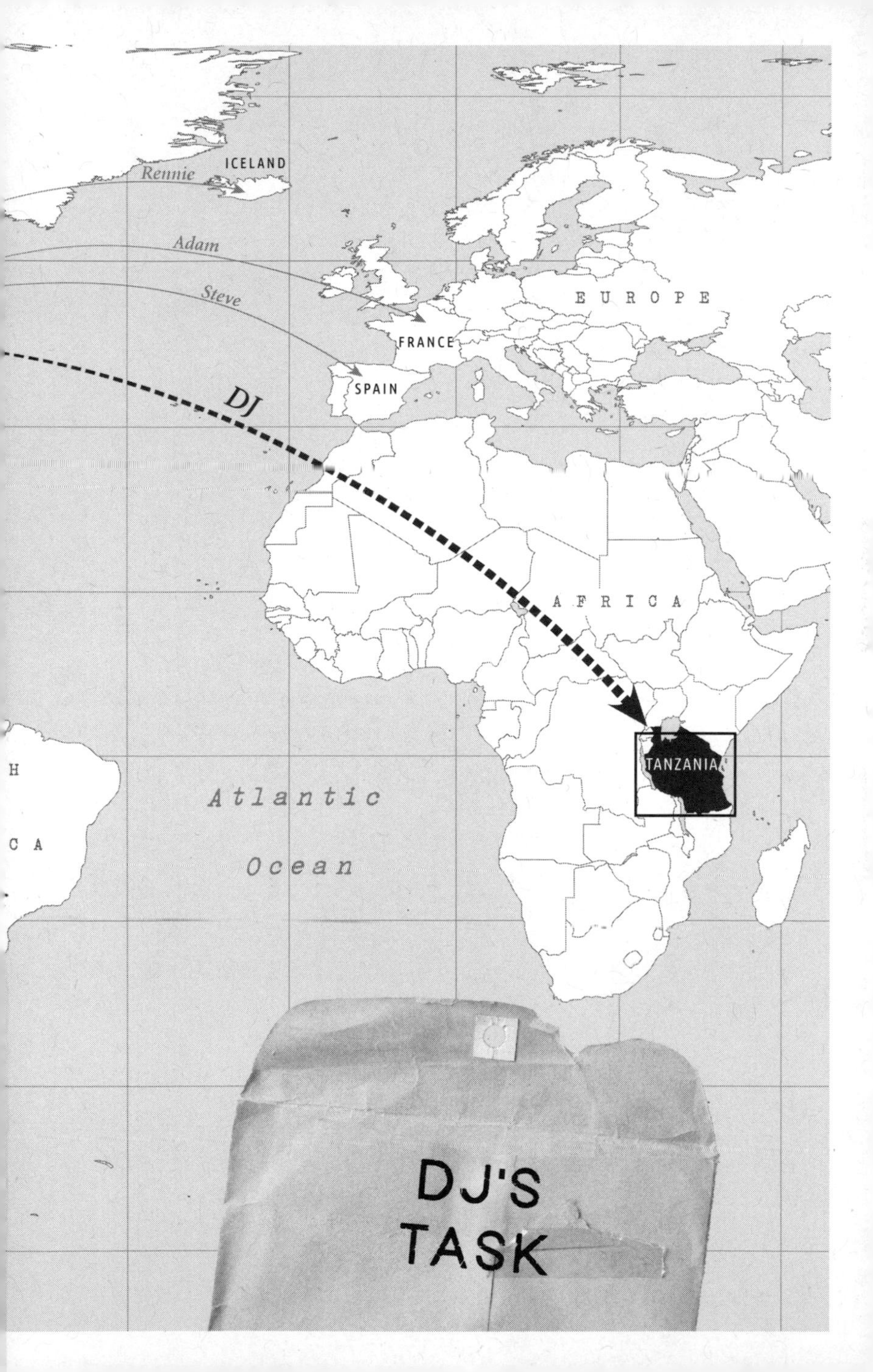
ICELAND
Rennie
Adam
Steve
EUROPE
FRANCE
SPAIN
DJ
AFRICA
TANZANIA
H
C A
Atlantic
Ocean
DJ'S
TASK

ONE

The room was large and lavish, with dark oak paneling. A big mahogany desk dominated the room; overstuffed leather chairs and couches encircled it. I'd never been in a lawyer's office before. But then again, prior to a few days ago, I'd never been in a funeral home or attended a funeral either.

There were twelve of us in the room—me, my mother, my brother Steve, my mother's three sisters and two of my uncles, and my four cousins, Adam, Webb, Spencer and Bernard, who insisted on being called Bunny. These were the eleven people in the world who meant the most to me. The only person missing was the reason we were here—my grandpa. A shudder radiated through my entire body. I hoped nobody saw it. My mother reached out and placed her hand on mine.

"It's all right, DJ," she said softly.

Her eyes were so red from crying. I knew how much she was going to miss him. I knew how much we were *all* going to miss him. I just couldn't afford to shed tears. Somebody had to be in control. That was my job.

His death had been hard on everybody, but maybe the hardest on my mother. I'd heard my Aunt Vicky talking about how we must be "reliving" my father's death. I thought that was a funny choice of words—how could a death be relived?—but I understood what she meant. That didn't mean I agreed with her, just that I understood. My father had been gone for so long, since I was really little, that I hadn't even been part of all of that. No funeral home, no visitation, no cemetery, no burial memories. I couldn't relive what I hadn't lived.

With my mother's whispered reassurance over, the room became completely silent again. It was almost as if all the oxygen had been sucked out of the room. Then again, since nobody seemed to be breathing, it wasn't like we needed air. We all just sat there, in silence, waiting for the lawyer to arrive. I didn't know what was in the will, and I didn't care what Grandpa was leaving me, because he'd already left so many memories. But it was a term of his will that we all needed to be there, so we had no choice. It would have been disrespectful for us not to come.

Of course that hadn't stopped my brother from trying to get out of it. Typical. If it wasn't his idea, he didn't want any part of it. Mom had finally convinced him. If she hadn't, I would have convinced him in a whole different way. Steve could be such a jerk sometimes. It was hard to believe that twins could be so different, but we rarely saw things the same way.

The silence seemed so *wrong*. Here we were, waiting to hear the will of a man who didn't believe in silence. He was always talking, telling stories, making jokes or singing songs. More than once, when he thought he was alone, I'd caught him humming or talking to himself. I'd even overheard him having both ends of a conversation and laughing at his own jokes. My mother always joked that he'd talk to a stone and get the stone to reply. That was just how he was. Wherever he went, he talked to complete strangers and they always talked back. He once said that strangers were just people he hadn't become friends with yet. He was so relentlessly friendly, so happy, so full of life. He *was* so full of life.

I hated seeing him in that coffin. The minister talked about how "lifelike" he looked lying there. That was garbage. That was the first time I'd ever seen him when he wasn't moving about. He was emotions in motion. He would jokingly say that he was what hyperactive kids grew up to be. He was what *I* would like to grow up to be, but that wasn't possible. For one thing, I don't have his way with people. He made everybody feel so comfortable. Total strangers felt like friends, friends felt like family, and family...well, he just made us feel like we were the most important people around. All of us. When people talked about tolerance for others, he bristled. He didn't believe in *tolerance*, he believed in *acceptance*.

Of course, I knew that everybody who was born died eventually, but I guess I didn't believe he would ever die. He told me he was going to live forever or die trying. He died trying. He was getting ready to put in a whole new garden. It was going to be more work than many men half his age could handle. He was looking forward to going to the cottage and having all of us up to visit. He kept saying he was going to water-ski this year. I knew he wasn't; he just said that to get his daughters all worried. Ninety-two-year-old men shouldn't be water-skiing.

A few nights ago he went to bed and woke up dead. I almost chuckled. He would have liked that—the rhyme of *bed* and *dead*, a little limerick in the making. One minute he was so full of life and the next—nothing. Everybody told us it was a wonderful way to go. No suffering. So for him, I was happy. But it just made it harder for the rest of us. We hadn't had time to adjust, to get used to the idea that he was gone. I still half expected him to walk into the room and—

The door opened and everybody turned as a man in a suit walked in.

"Good afternoon," he said as he settled in behind the desk.

There was a mumble of responses from across the room.

"Thank you for coming," he said. "My name is John Devine, and I've been David's lawyer for twenty years. This is a very sad day, and I must admit that this was a day I didn't expect to be part of. I'm much younger than David, but even so, I expected him to outlive me."

That comment generated smiles and nods.

"He was a man of so much passion. It was a true joy to have known him."

That was my grandpa. He *was* a joy.

"The terms of the will are both straightforward and, shall we say, most interesting." Mr. Devine paused and smiled. "And with a most interesting twist."

Interesting was such an interesting word. It could mean almost anything.

"Let's begin with the more conventional parts," he said. "All of David's assets—his home, investments and cottage—are to be divided equally among his daughters."

That was fair, and he was always fair.

"All of these assets, with the exception of the cottage, are to be liquidated and dispersed to the four heirs. The cottage's ownership will be transferred to list his daughters as co-owners. It says, and I quote, 'This was a place of so many great memories shared with my family that I wish it to be used in perpetuity by my grandchildren and their children and their children.'" He paused. "Is that all clear?"

There was a murmuring of agreement and nodding of heads. I was happy. Some of my best memories were from the cottage. Weekends and summers spent with all of my cousins and our parents and Grandpa.

"Excellent," Mr. Devine said. "Now I need to set out the next part—the interesting part—of the will. A sum of money—a rather substantial sum—has been put aside to fund an undertaking…or I should say, *seven* undertakings." He paused. "This is without a doubt one of the most unusual clauses that I have ever been asked to put in a will."

He looked slowly from person to person, deliberately pausing at each one. Everybody was staring directly at him, leaning forward in their seats. He certainly had everybody's complete, undivided attention—even Steve's.

Just read the thing, I thought.

"I know you are *all* anxious to hear about these undertakings. However, I cannot share them with all of you at this moment."

There was an eruption of confused protest.

"Please, please!" he said, cutting the protest short. "You will *all* be fully informed, but not all of you will be informed at the same time. Some people will have to leave the room prior to the undertakings being read."

I knew where this was going; he was going to ask the grandkids to leave. That wasn't fair. I understood the younger ones being asked to leave, but why me? I was almost eighteen—well, in a few months—and it wasn't like I wasn't mature enough to handle anything. And it wasn't as if my father was here to support my mother—that was my role. I should be allowed to stay even if the other five grandsons had to leave.

Mr. Devine continued. "Therefore, as per the terms of the will, I request that the grandsons—"

"I'm not going anywhere," Steve said.

Everybody turned to him.

"I don't want to be kicked out of the room," he reiterated.

"You'll go if you're told to go," I said forcefully.

"You don't understand," the lawyer said. "He *can* stay."

"If he's staying, then I'm staying as well," I said.

"And me too," added my cousin Webb.

The room erupted in protest again.

"Could everybody please just stop!" the lawyer yelled as he stood up. "Please, I am reading a will. Decorum is needed. Out of respect for the deceased, you all need to follow his directions. Is that understood?"

"Sorry," I said.

"Me too," my brother said.

I knew he meant it. He was impulsive and he could be a real pain. There were times I wanted to give him a smack—and had—but he *was* okay.

"Before I go on, I need to ask *everybody* to agree to respect the terms of his will—*all* the terms of his will."

"Of course we agree," my mother said.

My aunts and uncles all nodded in agreement.

"Excellent," the lawyer said. "Now, I need to have everyone except the six grandsons to leave the room."

"What?" one of my aunts exclaimed, voicing the disbelief we all felt.

"Did you say that the adults have to leave?" Aunt Debbie asked.

Mr. Devine nodded. "Yes. Everyone except the grandsons."

TWO

If it was eerie to be here to begin with, then it was even eerier to watch all our parents leave the room. My mother, the last to leave, hesitated at the door and we locked eyes.

"It's okay," I mouthed to her.

She smiled ever so slightly and closed the door, leaving the six of us alone with the lawyer.

"Well, gentlemen," he said, "I'm assuming that nobody saw this coming."

"Grandpa was always full of surprises," Bunny said.

"So I guess because of that we're *not* that surprised," Steve added.

"Interesting perspective," the lawyer said. "The only way you would have been surprised is if he didn't do something to surprise you."

"Pretty much," my brother agreed.

"So if he'd done nothing, then you would have actually been surprised, which wouldn't have been a surprise. Sort of a Catch-22, don't you think?"

"Do you think, sir, that we could go on?" I said. "I believe we're all anxious to hear what you're going to tell us."

"I'm sure you are," he said. "But, actually, *I'm* not going to tell you anything." He paused. "Your *grandfather* is."

Instantly, a bizarre thought popped into my head: maybe he wasn't dead. Maybe somehow this had been some sort of—

"I'm going to play a video your grandfather made," Mr. Devine said.

I felt my whole body sag. What else could it be? It was stupid of me even to think that he was still alive.

The lawyer walked over to a big cabinet that held a television. He turned to face us. "I was in the room when your grandfather recorded this. I think *all* of you will be at least a little surprised by what he has to say."

He clicked a remote, and the TV came to life. First it was blank, and then there was Grandpa!

"I'm not sure why I have to be wearing makeup," he said, turning to face somebody off camera. "This is my will, not some late-night talk show... and it's certainly not a *live* taping."

A couple of unseen people laughed, and then Grandpa turned to look directly into the camera.

"Good morning...or afternoon, boys," he began. "If you are watching this, I must be dead, although on this fine afternoon I feel very much alive."

I looked at him closely, trying to figure out when the video would have been made. He didn't look any different or younger than when I'd last seen him, so it wasn't that long ago, and I could tell it was recorded right here in this office. Somehow that made it seem more real and less real all at once.

I recognized his striped sweater—my mother had knit it for him. And, as always, he was wearing his black beret. It had been strange seeing him in the coffin without it, but apparently it was a term of the will that it wasn't buried with him. I wondered where it was.

"I want to start off by saying that I don't want you to be too sad. I had a good life and I wouldn't change a minute of it. That said, I still hope that you are at least a little sad and that you miss having me around. After all, I was one *spectacular* grandpa!"

We all started to laugh.

"And you were simply the best grandsons a man could ever have. I want you to know that of all the joys in my life, you were among my greatest. From the first time I met each of you to the last moments I spent with you—and of course I don't know what those last moments were, but I know they were wonderful—I want to thank you all for being part of my life. A very big, special, wonderful, warm part of my life."

He reached down and took a sip from a glass in front of him. His hand shook ever so slightly. His hands never shook; he was nervous.

"I wanted to record this rather than just have my lawyer read it out to you. Hello, Johnnie."

"Hello, Davie," the lawyer replied.

"Johnnie, I hope you appreciate that twenty-year-old bottle of Scotch I left you," Grandpa said. "And you better not have had more than one snort of it before the reading of my will!"

The lawyer held up two fingers.

"But knowing you the way I do, I suspect you would have had two."

The lawyer looked a bit embarrassed. "He did know me well," he said to us.

"I just wanted—needed—to say goodbye to all of you in person, or at least as in person as this allows." He took another sip from his glass. The hand was still shaking.

"Life is an interesting journey, one that seldom takes you where you think you might be going. Certainly I never expected that I was going to become an old man. In fact, there were more than a few times when I was a boy that I didn't believe I was going to live to see another day, never mind live long enough to grow old."

From the stories he'd told us, I knew how close he'd been to death on many occasions. He had been shot down when he was a pilot in World War II, and then he'd flown all over the world after that.

"But I did live a long and wonderful life. I was blessed to meet the love of my life, your grandmother Vera. It is so sad that she passed on before any of you had a chance to meet her. I know people never speak ill of the dead—and I'm counting on you all to keep up that tradition with me—but your grandmother was simply the most *perfect* woman in the world.

"Her only flaw, as far as I can see, was being foolish enough to marry me. She gave me not only a happy life, but four daughters...four amazing daughters. I just wish she could have been there to watch them grow into the four wonderful women who became your mothers."

My grandmother had died when our mothers were young—the youngest, Aunt Vicky, was only four at the time. My grandpa raised the girls on his own at a time when men didn't do that.

"I was always comforted by the thought that I believed she was watching them too. Sitting up there in heaven or wherever. I guess as you're hearing this, I have an answer to that question. I pray that I'm with her now."

He lifted up the glass again and made a little toast toward us. I noticed his hand wasn't shaking anymore. He was getting more comfortable, more relaxed. More like Grandpa.

"Being both father and mother to my girls meant that I was always running fast to try and do everything. Sometimes the need to earn a living got in the way of me being there for my daughters. There were too many school plays, violin recitals and soccer games that I never got to. And that was why I made a point to be there for almost every one of your games and school events and concerts," he said.

He *was* there for everything, always. Sitting in the bleachers screaming at the referees, or in the front row at the concerts, cheering and clapping, or right there by the bed when you woke up after having your tonsils out. He was just there.

"This was both a promise I made and a complete joy. You boys, you wonderful, incredible, lovely boys, have been such a blessing…seven blessings. Some blessings come later than others."

Seven? He meant six. There were six of us. He must have been even more nervous than he looked. His voice caught over the last few words, and I thought he was on the verge of crying. He took another sip from his glass. A long, slow sip.

"But I didn't bring you here simply to tell you how much I loved you all. Being part of your lives was one of the greatest achievements of my life, and I wouldn't trade it for anything, but being there for all your big moments meant that I couldn't be elsewhere. I've done a lot, but it doesn't seem that time is going to permit me the luxury of doing everything I wished for. So, I have some requests, some *last* requests."

We all looked at each other, questioningly.

"In the possession of my lawyer are some envelopes," he said. "One for each of you."

I turned around. Mr. Devine stood off to the side of the room. In his hand was a fan of envelopes.

"Each of these requests, these tasks," Grandpa continued, "has been specifically selected for you to fulfill. All of the things you will need to complete your task will be provided—money, tickets, guides. Everything."

Tickets and guides? What did he want us to do?

"I am not asking any of you to do anything stupid or unnecessarily reckless—certainly nothing as stupid or reckless as I did at your ages. Your parents may be worried, but I have no doubts. Just as I have no doubts that you will all become fine young men. I am sad that I will not be there to watch you all grow into the incredible men I know you will become. But I don't need to be there to know that will happen.

I am so certain of that. As certain as I am that I will be there with you as you complete my last requests, as you continue your life journeys."

He lifted up his glass.

"A final toast. To the best grandsons a man could ever have." He tipped back the glass and drained it. He put down the glass and stared directly into the camera. "I love you all so much. Good luck."

The screen went black. He was gone.

The lawyer turned off the TV. "In my hands are the seven envelopes. One for each grandson."

"You mean six," I said. "There are only six of us."

"Well, as I said, there is a most interesting twist. There *is* a seventh grandson."

THREE

I went up to my room and closed the door. I needed to be alone to process that last little piece of news. My grandpa had had another daughter—a daughter conceived, born and raised without his knowledge. That daughter, now dead, had a son named Rennie. My grandpa had only become aware of this extra grandson a few months ago. So there weren't six of us, there were seven. It was strange how this news had disturbed me but seemed to amuse Steve. That was so much like him.

And in my hand, along with the envelope from my grandpa, was information about his extra grandson.

Rennie was, almost to the day, the same age as me. There was a request from my grandpa, relayed through his lawyer, that we all contact Rennie so he'd feel more a part of our family. I'd do it, because Grandpa had asked me to, but not right now. First things first. I had to look at my task.

I sat on my bed in my room, alone. Alone was the only way to read this. I couldn't guarantee how I'd handle it, and I didn't want anybody to see me cry. I held the large manila envelope in my hand. It was thick, so obviously it contained more than a simple letter.

I turned the envelope around in my hands. My nickname—DJ—was typed on the front. Somehow it would have been more real if it was in his handwriting. Well, as real as any of this could be.

There was no point in looking at it any longer. Carefully I unsealed the top and looked inside. There was something soft and black—his beret! I pulled it out and couldn't help but smile. Pinned to it was a piece of paper with my name on it. He'd left it for me! That meant so much. Gently I placed it on my lap and then turned the envelope over and three smaller envelopes tumbled out. One said *1—Read Now* in big letters, another *2—Bottom.* What did that mean? The third had *3—End* written on it. All three were in his handwriting. It was like he'd heard that I didn't want them typed. Slowly, deliberately, carefully, I opened up the first envelope.

Dear DJ,

I remember the first time I ever held you—my first grandchild. You were no more than fifteen minutes old when your father placed you in my arms. Soon to be followed by your brother. I'd never held anybody so young—I didn't even hold any of my daughters that soon. Things were a little different in my day. I know you won't make that mistake with your children—you'll be right there with your wife. That's the right thing to do, and I know I can always count on you to do the right thing.

That made me smile. I always prided myself on doing the right thing, and my grandpa appreciated that.

It may sound strange to talk to you about a wife and children, but life all happens so quickly. It seems like only moments ago that I was like you—a teenager. And then it all happened so fast, from boy to young man, to man, to father, to grandfather to, well, a memory. You'll have to accept my apology for sounding both morbid and philosophical, but death tends to do that to a man.

Death...he was dead. I didn't know when he had written this, but it was the last thing he'd ever written just for me. Well, I guess technically the second and third letters would be the last, but still, I could appreciate being philosophic. I'd done a lot of thinking about life and death over the past few days.

I don't know what I expected the first time I held you, but it wasn't what I got. There was no crying or squirming from you. You were so calm—calmer than I was. You looked up at me, eyes wide, and I got the feeling you were studying me, trying to figure out who this old man was and what was going to happen next. And even stranger, I got the feeling that you almost had it figured out.

Your mother always said that you were an old soul. I know you've heard that so often, and at times it even made you bristle, but it's true. You were always the kid who did what he was supposed to do. From sleeping through the night, to toilet training, to learning to read, to being the captain of every team you ever played on. Most kids didn't know what was going on. Some of the smarter kids had questions. But you, well, you seemed to have the answers.

I also remember so clearly when your father died. It wasn't just the saddest day in your life, but one of the saddest in mine. I was powerless to protect either your mother or you or your brother from the pain. I saw you shed tears, but you were so strong. I think you helped your mother through it all more than I did. Let's be honest, I think you helped me.

Maybe that's where your old soul evolved into a leader. You became more than a child. You took care of your mother and your brother and then all of your cousins. I know that sometimes your brother and cousins may have resented having another "parent," but I know they respect you so much. I expect as each of you completes the requests I've made that there will be communication among the seven of you. I know you will be there to help the others fulfill their challenges, but also hope you'll be strong enough to accept their help too. A good leader knows when to follow, when to accept help, when to go to others for assistance.

I've always thought that the problems of the world were caused because we failed to understand one simple fact: we are all part of the same family. There are not different races of people but one race—the human race. If we were able to trace our lives back through the generations, we'd find the links that connect us all. There are people who speak about the Garden of Eden as if it was a fact, and others who see the theory of evolution as more than a theory. In some ways they're both correct. However, we all share the same beginnings. We started with one mother and father—one Adam and Eve—even if through evolution.

I know I've told you some of my tales from my time in Africa. I flew different types of small planes up and down the whole of East Africa. Those were times of adventure, abandon and excitement. It was where my soul was healed after the horror of war, where I became able to live and love again and go on with life.

Ashes to ashes, dust to dust—those words were said at my funeral. I believe them.

DJ, here is my request. I want some of my ashes returned to where it all began for mankind, but also where my life began again—to Africa, to the Rift Valley. I want you to go to Tanzania and climb Mount Kilimanjaro.

Some of my ashes have been placed in my walking cane. When you reach the top, scatter my ashes in the wind so that they can be blown throughout the valley and I can once again be reunited with my ancestors.

With my great thanks, and great love,

Grandpa

P.S. Say hello to Elijah for me—he will be there to meet you at the airport, take care of you and make all the arrangements for your trek up the mountain.

He wants me to climb a mountain to spread his ashes? I could hardly believe what I'd just read. I looked away from the envelope. Africa...I was going to Africa...to Tanzania to climb a mountain. I almost felt too stunned to think. But I needed to. I did a quick calculation in my head. My last exam was in three days. I would be starting football camp in August—on a full scholarship. Grandpa had been so proud. As long as I left right away, I'd have plenty of time to do this. After all, how long could it possibly take to climb a mountain?

FOUR

"Don't worry, you'll catch your flight," my mother said.

"I'm not worried," I replied. "It's just that for international flights I'm supposed to be there three hours early."

"We'll be there almost three hours early."

"What if there's a major traffic jam or we get a flat tire or—?"

"The roads are clear, and if we needed to, we'd fix the tire."

I sat back and tried to relax. Then again, I'd only be truly relaxed when I was on the plane coming back home, the wheels touching the ground and my task finished. It would take no more than seven or eight sleeps. That made me sound like a toddler, but that's how I always counted being away from home.

"It's going to be strange with both you and your brother gone. I'm going to be worried."

"There's nothing to be worried about," I offered. "Remember, Steve is just going to Spain."

"So I should be worried about you and that mountain?" she asked.

"You don't need to be worried about *either* of us. It's going to be a walk in the park."

"Climbing a mountain is hardly a walk in the park," she said.

"No, actually it is. Kilimanjaro is in a national park. How dangerous can a park be?" I joked. She didn't laugh, so obviously she didn't think my little joke was funny.

"Steve leaves soon, right?"

"The day after you." My mother chuckled. "Your brother reminds me so much of your grandpa."

"Steve? He's *nothing* like Grandpa."

"Your grandpa mellowed with age, but think of the stories he told from when he was young. I think that's why the two of them never got along as well as he did with the others. Your grandpa saw too much of himself in Steve and wanted to try to change him so he wouldn't go through the same grief."

"Grief?" I asked.

"I often wonder what all those adventures of Grandpa's were about. I know the war was hard on him, and I wonder if he was trying to find himself," she said.

"And what is Steve trying to find?"

"Maybe the same thing. Peace."

I didn't think Steve would ever find anything except more grief. Well, at least he was an expert at finding and giving it. He was my twin brother, and I loved him, but there were times I could have killed him. We were so different—even physically. I towered over him and must have outweighed him by ten kilograms. I loved sports, and he had no interest in them whatsoever. History was one of his passions, and the only history I cared about was the score in yesterday's games.

"I'll try to keep in touch by texting you when I'm gone. Can you keep an eye on everybody for me?"

I asked. "You know—all the guys—to make sure they follow their tasks."

"Don't worry, I'm sure everybody will be fine." She paused. "Are you going to contact Rennie?"

"That's what Grandpa asked us to do, so I'll do it. It's just so...so..."

"Yes, it is. I can only imagine the shock your grandfather felt when he found out he had another daughter and a seventh grandson."

"Yeah, I guess." I didn't want to think about that right now. "I just want to make sure they'll all be okay," I said. "I'm a little worried about Bernie."

"Bunny will do just fine."

"*Please* don't call him that," I said.

"Bunny is what he calls himself. It's cute."

"It was cute when he was four. He's fifteen and in high school."

"Well, I remember somebody who used to walk around in a little tiger suit," my mother said.

"I was three, not fifteen. How cute would it have been if I wore it to high school? And at least I wanted to be a tiger and not a bunny."

"He likes being called Bunny," she said.

"It doesn't matter what he likes. Being called Bunny is the sort of thing that gets him picked on all the time."

"I know your aunt is grateful for the help you've given him."

"I've tried. As long as I'm there, nobody really dares to pick on him much, but next year I'm not gonna be around. It's not like Spencer is going to step in." Spencer was Bunny's "big" brother, but he wasn't very big and wasn't much less of a target than Bunny.

"He might," she said.

"It's not the same. Nobody in the world is afraid of Spencer."

She laughed. "I'm just glad my little *Tigger* has always been there to take care of his little cousin Bunny, the way Tigger took care of Winnie-the-Pooh."

There was nobody else in the car, so calling me Tigger, her special name for me, was okay. It wasn't so okay when Steve called me that, especially in public.

"You are a very hard act to follow," my mother said.

"What?"

"Sometimes I think your cousins feel like they can't hope to compete with you."

"It's not a competition," I said.

My mother laughed. "I never thought I'd hear you say the words *not* and *competition* in the same sentence."

"I just try to do my best, that's all. The point of a game is to win, but I am a good loser too."

"And how much practice have you had at being a loser?"

"I'll try to lose more in the future."

"Losing isn't the end of the world."

"I never said it was." Although it had felt like it the few times it happened.

We circled around the ring road leading to the terminal.

"Are you sure you don't want me to come inside?" my mother asked.

"No need for you to spend money on parking. I'll be fine."

She slowed down and pulled into an open spot. I got out quickly, and she popped open the trunk. I grabbed my green duffel bag and my backpack and of course my grandpa's cane with his remains in a secret compartment inside. I held it tightly.

"Are you sure you have everything?" she asked.

"Everything."

"I'm not even sure why I asked. You are the most responsible seventeen-year-old in the world." She paused. "But I'm still going to be worried until you get back."

"Funny, but I'm going to be worried about *you* until I get back."

She started to tear up. I felt tears start to surface, but I blinked them away. I couldn't let her see me cry or let her know that I was worried.

"I better get inside and check in," I said.

She threw her arms around my neck. She was small but strong. I gave her a big hug back.

"I love you," she said.

"Yeah, I sort of figured that. I *am* pretty loveable."

She made a huffing sound in my ear.

"I know, I know, Mom. I love you too, but I have to go."

She squeezed a little tighter before letting go.

"I'll text you as soon as I'm on the ground," I said. I reached out and gave her another hug and then walked toward the terminal. I stopped, turned around and waved. She waved back, and then I went inside.

Now that she was gone, I could let my defenses down a bit, although I didn't want to cry in front of strangers either. I was worried. More than that, I was scared. I was traveling halfway around the world, by myself, to climb a mountain. A really big mountain. Maybe I should be scared. I just couldn't let anybody know.

I had one thing to do before I checked in. I pulled out my phone and sent a text to my cousins.

`Hey guys. Just getting on plane to Tanzania. Good luck to all. Back soon. Text if you need help. Don't let Grandpa down.`

I pushed *Send*, knowing that almost instantly all six would get my message. Each of us had an individual task to complete, but somehow it felt like it was up to *me* to make sure they were all completed. But I'd have to finish my own task before I could help anybody else.

It was just me—me and Grandpa's cane. It was made of smooth brown wood and the handle was two carved elephants, their tusks intertwined. I thought back to him, cane in hand, walking, or leaning on it, sometimes spinning it around or using it as a dancing partner as he did a little jig, his ever-present black beret tipped to one side. I gave the cane a little shake and I could feel the ashes shifting inside. This cane was such a part of him. Now *he* was part of *it*. Here, in my hands.

FIVE

My eyes jerked open as the plane's wheels hit the runway. We bounced up and down a few times, and then finally stuck to the ground. We rolled along the runway. It was so rough, I wondered if we'd landed in a field. I looked out the window. The runway was a narrow strip of pavement lined on both sides by dense bush. Probably good that I'd been asleep as we approached the airstrip and hadn't seen it coming. I was just glad to be back on the ground.

I really didn't like flying at all. It wasn't just about being up high, which I didn't like. To me, flying was less like science and more like magic.

How could a plane hang up there in the air? I knew all about aerodynamics, but it still didn't feel right to me.

I'd never told anybody about my fear of flying. Particularly Grandpa. He loved flying almost more than anything else. I remember being up in a plane with him behind the wheel. He loved being up there, and I loved being with him, so I made sure he didn't know how much I hated flying. He'd put me in the copilot seat when I was so small I could hardly see out through the windscreen. Sometimes he'd even let me put my hands on the rudder—a four-year-old flying a plane.

While we flew, he told stories: flying in his Lancaster during the war, being a bush pilot in the North, bouncing around Africa. That made me smile. When I thought about the last time he was in the air at the controls of his plane, my smile left. He knew he was getting too old to fly solo, and that wasn't just his thinking but the government's. As he'd said, "Regulations are regulations, and I can't fight them." So he allowed his pilot's license to lapse.

I had been there on the ground, holding my mother's hand, Steve holding the other, when Grandpa landed that last time. He went up alone, just him and the plane and the sky.

If I closed my eyes, I could still see him slowly walking away from the plane after he landed. He told me it was one of the saddest days of his life. I was sad for him, but secretly I was grateful I'd never have to go up with him again. And that *still* made me feel guilty.

I was now on the third flight of my trip and each plane had gotten smaller and more suspect. Finally we arrived in Moshi, a town near Kilimanjaro. Grandpa would have loved this last plane because it was so tiny. It held only sixteen people and seemed less like a plane than a bus with two propeller-driven engines. Bad enough that it was like a bus, but it wasn't even a *nice* bus. The carpeting on the floor was worn and torn, as were the seats. Torn wouldn't have been bad if my seat hadn't also been crooked—one of the support legs was busted—and if it had a seat belt that worked. Rather than buckling up, the attendant had helped me tie the two ends together.

The plane was still bumping along the runway when people started to get up from their seats. They seemed to have no sense of safety or following rules, although I could appreciate wanting to get off this plane as fast as possible. On the ground was good, but *feet* on the ground was better. I thought the flight attendant would tell them to sit down, but she hadn't bothered. Passengers held on to seats, swaying while they opened up the overhead compartments and pulled out their bags.

The plane finally came to a complete stop, and I untied my seat belt and got to my feet, smacking my head loudly against the overhead compartment. The thud was loud enough that people turned to stare. A few looked like they were about to laugh or giggle, and others looked concerned.

"I'm okay," I said to everybody and nobody. "They just don't make these big enough for me."

I stepped into a gap in the aisle and stood up, almost straight. My head brushed against the ceiling of the plane. I looked up and down the aisle. I was clearly the tallest person aboard. I pulled out my carry-on bag and then Grandpa's cane.

The door popped open, and sunlight and fresh air flooded in. I took a deep breath. It felt good. The first passengers exited, and the rest of us shuffled forward until I climbed off the plane and took my first step in Tanzania. I was here, and that meant I was one-third of the way to finishing my task.

I'd divided it into three parts: flying to Tanzania, climbing the mountain, and flying home. I figured the mountain part wouldn't take much longer than the flights.

I followed the little stream of passengers toward a small building, hoping they knew where they were going. Right inside the doors were the customs booths. One had a sign above it that read *East African Passports.* The other said *All Other Passports.* That was me.

I dug out my passport and went to the back of the line. There were three other people in front of me: two men in their twenties, and a much older woman. Maybe she was the mother of one of them, which reminded me: I'd have to text Mom and let her know I'd arrived.

The men stepped up to the customs booth, leaving just me and the older woman. She turned around to face me.

"First time in Tanzania?" she asked. She had a British accent.

I nodded. "Is it yours?"

"Yes," she replied. "Are you here to climb the mountain?"

"Yes. And you?"

"The plan is for me to—"

"Next!"

We both turned toward the customs booth. The guard was waving for her to come forward.

"Good luck with your climb," she said as she stepped up to the booth.

I didn't think luck was going to have anything to do with it.

I was hot and tired, and my legs were a little shaky. It had been almost twenty-four hours since my mother had dropped me off at the airport, and I hadn't gotten any more than two or three hours sleep since then. Fear of flying will do that to you.

The woman moved through customs, and I stepped forward.

"Passport, please," the official said.

He opened it up at the picture and held it up, looking from it to me.

"This is you?" he asked.

The question threw me. "Yeah, of course."

"It does not look so much like you," he said. "But many of you tourists look the same. Length of stay?"

"Two or three days."

"Why so short?"

"That should be long enough to climb the mountain," I answered.

"And you think you can do that in two days?"

"Well, I don't know; that's why I said maybe three."

He shook his head and gave me a look like I'd offended him.

"How much currency do you have?" he asked.

"Currency?"

"How much money do you have with you?"

I'd heard about this. He was asking me for a bribe. "I have enough," I said.

"Enough? Are you being insolent with me, young man?" he demanded. "I will ask you one more time, how much money do you have on you?"

His loud words and hard stare left me no doubt that I'd have to tell him and give him a bribe if he asked for it.

"Um…I'm not sure. I know I have enough. I have a couple of hundred dollars in US funds and lots of Tanzanian shillings and a bank card. Everything else is already paid for."

"You are traveling by yourself and you are only seventeen," he said. "Who will care for you when you are here?"

"I'm meeting a man named Elijah. He's probably out there waiting for me," I said, gesturing to the door with the Exit sign above it.

"What is this Elijah's last name? What is his occupation? Is he Tanzanian? Does he run a tour group?"

"I don't know."

"None of it?" he asked in disbelief. "You do not even know his full name?"

I shook my head.

"And you just trust that this Elijah will be out there waiting," he said. "What if he isn't? Do you have a number to contact him?"

Again I shook my head. I didn't feel good about that myself. I had just trusted that Grandpa and his lawyer had made all the arrangements.

"So if he is not there, what will you do?" he asked.

"I'm sure he is, but if he isn't, I guess I'll just wait."

"For how long?"

"Until he comes."

"And what if he does not come until tomorrow or the next day? Do you think this is a hotel where you can sleep?"

"I'm sure he'll be there."

He muttered something under his breath. I didn't need to know Swahili to know he was neither pleased nor impressed with me or my plan.

"Do you have anything to declare?" he asked. "Are you bringing in drugs or guns or alcohol or prohibited fruit or vegetables?"

Of course I wasn't bringing in any of those things, but I'd been told by the lawyer, Mr. Devine, that it was illegal to transport human remains across national borders. That was why they were hidden inside my grandpa's cane.

"Well?" he demanded.

"Um...no," I stuttered. Lying never came naturally to me.

"Then why did you not answer immediately?"

"I didn't understand you!"

"Why, is my English not *good* enough for you?" he snapped.

"I'm tired. Really tired. I don't have any of those things. I don't even drink and I'd never do drugs, and I don't have any weapons...anywhere."

He looked at me long and hard, as if he was trying to make a final decision about whether or not he should let me into the country. That made no sense. I was pretty sure there was no way he couldn't let me in. His scowl deepened, and then he picked up a stamp and thumped it against my passport and handed it back.

"I can go?"

"You sound surprised. Did you think you should be turned away?"

"Of course not!"

"Then leave and stop holding up the line."

As I fumbled with my passport and duffel bag and backpack, the cane slipped from my hand and fell to the floor. I bent over to pick it up.

"That is an interesting walking stick," he said.

"Thanks."

"Most people *leave* with such things. They do not bring them into the country."

"It's special. It belonged to my grandfather."

"Let me see," he said, holding out his hands.

Reluctantly I handed it to him.

"This design is local, carved by the Chagga people. I am Chagga."

"My grandpa spent some time right here when he was young, a long time ago. He was a pilot."

He turned the cane over in his hands, examining it with the same intensity he'd reserved for me. I had to resist the urge to grab it away from him. It wasn't just my grandpa's cane he was holding in his hands, it was my *grandpa*.

"This stick it is very light. As if…as if…" He shook the cane, and I could *feel* the ashes moving inside. "As if it were *hollow*."

He took the top and twisted it around until it popped open. He looked inside, and then looked up at me. "You thought you could fool me."

"I wasn't trying to fool you. It's just that—"

"It is a serious offence to smuggle drugs."

"Drugs!"

He yelled something in a language I couldn't understand, and before I could object, two men in uniforms, carrying guns, grabbed me!

SIX

I sat on the little bunk, legs up, arms around them, back against the rough wall. I looked down at my wrist for the time and was frustrated. They'd taken my watch and everything in my pockets, as well as my belt, my hiking boots and my socks. What did they think I was going to do with socks? Ball them up and throw them at the guards? How long had it been? One hour…two? And more importantly, how long would it be? They couldn't just keep me here. They'd soon discover that it wasn't drugs. But then again, it wasn't legal to transport human remains either. How long could I get sent to jail for doing that?

I heard the sound of footsteps and looked through the bars, past the two seated guards. Another soldier appeared, and the two guarding me rose to their feet and saluted. Whoever he was, he outranked them. From his tone, I could tell he was giving orders. He turned and stormed away, and they quickly unlocked my cell.

I got to my feet, sockless, scared and feeling very alone. I wished somebody—my mother, my grandpa, even one of my cousins—was here to help me. I had to get the cane back.

"Come," one of the guards said. His voice was soft, which only put me on high alert. I walked out of the cell.

"Wait!" he called out, and I froze.

The other guard ran off and returned a few seconds later carrying a pair of sandals. "Here, for you."

Confused, I took them from him. They were brown and worn out and obviously way too small for me. I put them on, though, and followed the guards down a hall to an empty room with rows of wooden chairs, a couple of tables and a big raised bench. A courtroom! Was I going to be put on trial? I spun around to face the guards, who both smiled at me. What was going on?

A door at the side of the room opened, and two more soldiers entered. Neither of *them* was smiling. Behind them came an older man dressed in a suit and carrying my grandpa's cane! He nodded in my direction, and my guards jumped to attention and saluted.

I expected the man to go and sit up at the judge's bench, but instead he came directly to me.

"Good afternoon," he said. "I believe this is yours." He offered me the cane.

Was this a trick? Was this his way of making me admit that it was mine? What was the point in arguing? We all knew it was mine. I took it.

"Thanks." It felt good to have it back, no matter what happened next.

"Would you like something to eat, or perhaps a drink? Tea or coffee or a soda?"

How strange and nice. I guess they did court differently here. "No...no, thank you, sir."

"I think I would like a tea. It would feel rude to drink alone, so I will ask them to bring enough if you change your mind. Do you like milk and sugar in your tea?"

"Um...yes, please...milk and lots of sugar."

He turned to two of the soldiers. "Could you please arrange for refreshments?"

"Yes, sir, Your Honor, Judge!" one said, and they saluted and left.

So he *was* a judge.

"Young David. I must apologize for keeping you waiting," he said.

I startled at the mention of my name—hardly anybody called me David—but how did he even know my name? Then I realized that of course he knew my name; they had my passport.

"I was delayed and could not be here for your arrival as planned," he said.

As planned? What did that mean?

He shook his head slowly. "I can so clearly see the resemblance. There is so much of him in you."

"Resemblance?" What did that mean? "Wait... are you Elijah?"

He laughed. "Oh, I am so sorry, I thought you knew that! I am indeed Elijah!"

"But he called you Your Honor."

"I am both your grandfather's friend Elijah and a judge. The reason I was delayed was that I was presiding over a court hearing in the capital city,

Dar es Salaam, where I sit on the bench of the Supreme Court of Tanzania."

"The Supreme Court...wow!"

He shrugged. "There are nine of us, so it is not just me. I hope you hold no hard feelings toward the customs officer; he was acting in accordance with his position. In fact, I spoke to him and commended him for his perceptiveness in discovering that the walking stick was hollow. That was most impressive, do you not agree?"

"I guess it was."

"Smuggling is a problem. Of course your grandfather's ashes do resemble drugs."

"Am I in trouble for bringing those in?"

He shook his head. "No. I am a judge with the Supreme Court. Minor issues of violating the law can be overlooked or forgotten completely. Did your grandfather ever tell you about his time in Tanzania?"

"He flew out of this airport, right?"

"It was more a dirt strip and hangar back then. Your grandfather, Davie, flew throughout this region. He was a very good man. Do you know the history of our country?"

"I know some things," I said. "This was a colony, right?"

"The joke in Tanzania is that all of Africa was much like Mount Kilimanjaro: white at the top and black underneath. We were ruled by the whites and were given few rights or freedoms. We were second-class people in our own country."

I had the urge to apologize, as if it was my fault because I was white.

"But your grandfather was different. He treated everybody with respect—even me, just a young boy when I knew him. He said he fought in wars, risking his life for freedom and democracy, and he wasn't going to be part of taking *anybody's* freedom. It is because of him I became a judge."

"That's amazing."

"And I mean not just because of what he meant, but because he provided the funds for my education."

"He did?"

"Each year there was an anonymous donor who paid for my education. To the very end, in our last letters, he still would not acknowledge that it was he." He paused. "But I knew. Does any of this surprise you?"

"No, that's what he was like."

"I will tell you a story. As a boy, to help my family I did work for some white people who lived here. I labored at their estate, and when I finished, the man paid me only half of what he had promised. When I objected, I was beaten."

"That's awful."

"Your grandfather saw the bruises. He stormed off, saying he was going to give the man a thrashing, but we stopped him, begging him to not go. Your grandfather was so big he could have given him a beating, but that white man was important and he would have had your grandfather arrested or forced to leave the country. It took a great deal of time to convince him not to act. Then he got an idea. Instead of beating him, he befriended this man."

"Why would he do that?"

"To gain his trust. He then offered, for a small price, to take him for a flight. The man was a braggart, so full of boastfulness, and happily went along." Elijah leaned forward. "I must tell you that I am afraid of flying," he said in a low voice. "That is why I drove here instead of flying. Thank goodness you have no such fears, or you would not be here."

I knew those fears better than I'd ever admit.

"So your grandfather took him for a flight that involved rapid rises and falls, near misses with trees or the mountainside, and flying upside down!"

I could absolutely picture my grandfather doing that.

"When they landed, the white man was covered with his own vomit, was even *whiter* than usual, and collapsed to the ground. It was more of a beating than he had given me!" Elijah burst into laughter, as if it was happening again before his eyes. "Afterward your grandfather gave me the money the man had given him for the flight. It was much more than what the man owed me, but your grandfather insisted."

He laughed once again, and I laughed along with him.

"Your grandfather was larger than life. I could tell you so many stories...many of which have nothing to do with such noble things. That man could get into more arguments—fights even—and he could drink more than any man I ever met!"

"Grandpa?" I questioned. "He didn't drink."

"When he first came here, if he wasn't flying, he was drinking, but in the end he did not drink any alcohol," Elijah said.

"I wonder what changed."

"He told me that he no longer *needed* to drink."

I thought back to Grandpa's letter to me—that's what he meant when he talked about his "soul being healed."

One of the soldiers returned carrying a tray.

"It is now time for me to repay some of my debt to him. While you are here, you will be under the care of my son, who is also named Elijah. He operates a tour company, and he will take you to the top of the mountain. Very exciting. Some day I might make the climb myself."

"You've never been up?" I blurted out without thinking.

"Never. Nor had your grandfather."

I hadn't even thought about that.

"Not that he did not try," Elijah said, "but he was not able to complete the climb, to reach the summit."

"That's hard to believe," I said.

"Yes, it is," he agreed. "He was a man of such strength and determination that it would seem that he could accomplish any goal. But that mountain... it has its way, and for some people it is harder. That is how it was for him. Now, do you wish to have tea?"

"Yes, that would be nice, thanks."

He poured tea into a cup and handed it to me.

"It would have been fitting for me to make the climb with you. A final honor to your grandfather, but I cannot. I must rush back to make my ruling in the case. I leave you in good hands. I will be here when you return. Now, let us finish our tea and then continue on our journey."

SEVEN

We walked out of the building and onto the streets. The sun was hot and the air dry. It felt good to be outside again. It felt good to be *free.*

The street was crowded with people and vehicles. The vehicles swerved and swirled with no regard to any rules of traffic, and it seemed as if they barely followed the laws of physics and gravity.

Almost directly in front of the building was a large shiny black car with dark tinted windows. It seemed strangely out of place. A chauffeur stood at its side.

"It seems most fitting that your grandfather chose the mountain for you. Do you know of its important place in our independence?"

"No...sorry."

"No need to be sorry. It is sad, but many Tanzanians do not seem to know either. In 1961 we gained our independence from England. Our first president, Mr. Julius Nyerere, ordered that a delegation bring wood to the top of the mountain to light a pyre. He said, 'We will light a candle on top of Mount Kilimanjaro which will shine beyond our borders, giving hope where there is despair, love where there is hate, and dignity where before there was only humiliation.'"

"That's amazing," I said.

"He was a great man. That fire no longer burns up there, but it still burns here," he said, touching his chest. "It is men like our first president, and your grandfather, who guide me as I try to sit in judgment while not being judgmental. We have, as a country, a distance yet to travel, but we will surely arrive."

His words sent a chill down my spine. "That sounds so much like something my grandpa would say."

He placed a hand on my shoulder. "That is a high compliment. Now let me bring you to my son.

It is only a short walk in that direction," he said, pointing up the road. "I will have my driver take us."

He gestured toward the big black car and the chauffeur.

"That's your car?" I gasped.

"It belongs to the government. I feel embarrassed. Why should there be such expensive cars for judges when some of our children go to sleep without food, go to school without shoes and have to study with so few books? They tell me that a judge must present as having authority, and this car is part of that authority, but I do not believe a man needs symbols such as that to represent authority."

He said something in Swahili to the driver, and they began a discussion that sounded very much like an argument.

"Is something wrong?" I asked.

"My friend here insists that we must leave for the capital immediately. He has been my driver for so long that he sometimes thinks he's my mother!"

"Thank goodness I am not!" the driver exclaimed in English. "It is enough work trying to be your driver without being your mother, but we do need to leave immediately in order to be *just* late instead of *very* late!"

"I know you are only trying to take care of me, my friend, but it is a very short drive, a minor detour," Elijah said.

"It is not the drive, but the delay when we get there. You will need to talk to every person. It could take *hours.* Hours that we do not possess."

"If it isn't far, I could just walk," I said.

"It is just up the road," the driver replied.

"No, no," Elijah objected. "It would not be right for him to walk."

"And would it be right if you did not render a verdict in the trial today?" the driver asked. "Are you not the one who always says that justice delayed is justice denied?"

Elijah laughed. "It is not my quote, but those are my words. I am surprised that you listen so closely."

"We *all* listen to your words, sir."

"Why don't I just walk? My stuff isn't heavy." I held up my bag, my hiking boots tied to it. In my hand I held the walking stick. I was wearing my backpack. I realized that I was still wearing the jail sandals. I'd forgotten about them.

He looked hesitant.

"I came to climb the mountain, so walking up the street shouldn't be too hard," I said.

"Now *you* are sounding like your grandfather. It is just up the street. The sign reads *East Africa Walking Tours*. My son expects you."

We shook hands. His driver opened the back door of the car and Elijah climbed in, the door closing behind him.

"Thank you for understanding," the driver said. "He is a *great* man, but more important, he is a *good* man."

He got in and they drove off quickly, leaving behind a cloud of dust that engulfed me. I watched as the car drove away, leaving me alone. Well, alone except for hundreds of people, all of whom seemed to be looking at me. There was no point in just standing there being stared at.

I turned and started to walk and then just stopped, stunned. For the first time I saw it—Mount Kilimanjaro. It rose up, filling the horizon, dominating the sky. There were shades of green at the bottom, giving way to browns and blacks. The top was white, crowned with snow and ice.

It looked gigantic, and for the first time I had doubts. Could I do this? I pushed those doubts away.

I started to cross the road and then stopped myself as a vehicle whipped by, inches from my face. The roadway was crowded with vehicles moving wildly and randomly. This wasn't going to be easy. There was a slight gap in traffic, and I dodged across the street, slipping between a dilapidated-looking little bus overflowing with people, the roof piled high with cargo, and a big four-wheel-drive SUV full of white people who were probably here to climb the mountain.

I got well off to the side of the road, away from the ongoing rush of a truck that roared by, fouling the air with the heavy smell of its thick blue exhaust fumes. That was only one of the smells that filled the air. The other was smoke, which came from the fires of the roadside food sellers and from piles of burning garbage. I didn't like the smell, but at least something was being done with the litter that covered the side of the road.

As I crossed the road, I couldn't help but think that the vehicles on the road pretty well summed up the extremes of this town: the mostly white tourists, who wore expensive safari clothing and thick hiking boots, and the locals, all of whom were black. The adults were dressed in everything from fancy dresses to suits with shiny shoes. Some of the children were shoeless and dressed in rags. I thought of what Elijah had said about Tanzania: white at the top and black underneath.

Lining the street were stores and ramshackle little stalls selling trinkets and souvenirs. It seemed like they were all selling the same things: beads and necklaces, carvings of African animals, spears and arrows, and shields, as well as postcards. Most prominent of all were the T-shirts that proudly read *I Climbed Kili!* I couldn't help but wonder how hard the climb could be if they mass-produced a T-shirt bragging about it.

People at the stalls kept calling out for me. "Hey, *mzungu*...come in...good deals!" *Mzungu* was one of the few Swahili words I knew; it meant white man. Did they really think that calling me *mzungu* would impress me? My few other Swahili words were *jambo*, which meant hello, *samba*, which was lion, *rafiki* for friend, and *hakuna matata*, which meant no worries. It was probably not a good sign that the movie *The Lion King* was the source of my limited vocabulary.

In among the little stalls and stores were kids, some as young as seven or eight, begging me for a "few shillings." Most were polite enough, but a couple yelled out things as I passed. It might be just as well that I didn't know much Swahili. I walked, eyes straight ahead, trying to just ignore them all. I couldn't give money to all of them. Besides, my money was all safely hidden away in the money belt around my waist. Nobody was going to get my money. It was safe, right? I slowly raised my free hand and inconspicuously pressed it against my side so I could feel the money belt. It was still there.

The street was slightly uphill. It wasn't steep and it wasn't long, but strangely I could feel it in my lungs. I felt myself slow down slightly. I guessed jet lag and lack of sleep were having a bit of an effect. At the same time I was beginning to wish I'd brought less stuff. I'd tried to pack light, but now I wished I'd packed even lighter. Between the pack on my back, the bag in my hand and, of course, the cane, I had too much.

Just up ahead I caught sight of a little boy flitting through the traffic. He couldn't have been any older than five, and the only thing the vehicles did was honk at him rather than slow down. Somehow he made it across the road without getting squashed, but then he fell down and started to cry! He was wailing away like he'd been hit. I rushed over.

"Are you okay, little guy?"

He looked up, his eyes got wide, and he cried louder! Then I saw why. He'd ripped open his knee somehow, and it was bleeding.

"Let's see if we can fix this."

He looked scared. I flashed him a big smile. "I'm going to *help*." I said the word *help* louder and slower.

I set down my bag, hauled off my pack and crouched down beside him.

"I've got a first-aid kit," I explained, although I got the feeling he didn't understand English. I showed him the plastic case with the big red cross on the top. Maybe that symbol was part of a universal language.

"I'll fix that up," I said, pointing at his bleeding knee. "I'm trained in first aid."

He stopped crying. Maybe he did understand. I pulled out some gauze, a cotton ball and a bottle of hydrogen peroxide to wash away any germs. I soaked the cotton ball with the antiseptic.

"This is going to sting," I said. Of course he didn't understand. "It will be...ouch!" I said, pretending to touch the ball with a finger. He giggled.

I took the ball and started to rub. He grimaced and pulled away a little bit but didn't cry or scream out. I washed away any germs. Next I took the piece of gauze and taped it in place with two pieces of adhesive tape.

"There you go."

"*Assante*," he said, his voice just a whisper, the catch of tears still sounding in his throat.

I smiled. I knew that word too. *Assante*—thank you.

"*Karibo*. You're welcome," I replied and he smiled back.

He got up and walked off with just a little limp. He'd probably have a good story to tell about how some big *mzungu* fixed him up.

I turned to put my first-aid kit away, but where was my pack? It had been right here beside me. I looked up and saw a boy running off with it!

"Hey!" I yelled as I jumped to my feet. "Stop that boy!"

He scampered through the crowded street, and I ran after him. Stupid sandals. Why hadn't I changed into my running shoes or hiking boots? Wait—what about my other bag? I looked back in time to see another boy making off with it and the cane… the cane with my grandfather's ashes in it! I skidded to a stop and started after him.

"Stop him, he's got my things!" I screamed.

A few people turned and looked, but nobody tried to stop him. I'd have to get him myself. He had a good lead, but he wasn't big and the bag was heavy, and what he didn't know was that I was an athlete—an athlete wearing too-small sandals. I scrunched my toes together to try to keep them on my feet, but I couldn't pick up any speed or gain any ground. I wasn't going to catch him wearing these things. I kicked them off and kept running in my bare feet. The ground was hard but level enough, and I was starting to gain on him when—

"Agghhh!" I screamed as something stuck into my foot.

I hopped forward for a couple of steps, grabbing my hurt foot before I realized that I didn't have time to look at it if I wanted to get my stuff back. I took another step and felt a stab of pain shoot into my foot, but I didn't stop. I'd played football with worse pain than this.

Up ahead the kid disappeared and reappeared as he wove through the crowd. I was gaining but not fast. My legs felt dead and my feet heavy, and I was struggling to get my breath. I had to catch him soon. I was getting closer and closer.

He made a quick turn and vanished behind a building. I reached the corner and he was gone! I looked around. He wasn't there. Nobody was there. I was standing alone in the little alley. The kid was gone. My stuff was all gone. The cane containing my grandfather's ashes was gone.

I doubled over, hands on my knees, straining to get my breath, my lungs burning. I was shaking and sweating and I felt like I might throw up. But feeling sick wasn't the worst thing. The worst thing was that I'd failed. I'd lost the cane. I wouldn't be able to fulfill my grandpa's last request, and everybody would know it. What would my mother think...my brother...my whole family? Wait...nobody would have to know. I could just tell them that I did it.

Nobody would ever question that I'd succeeded. It was just assumed I would. Nobody would know except for me. And Grandpa. He'd know.

And then I saw the cane, peeking out at me from a patch of rough ground and weeds where the thief must have dropped it. I went over and picked it up. I'd never been so happy to see anything in my whole life.

I looked skyward. "Thank you. I'm sorry. It won't leave my hand again."

I walked out of the alley, short of breath, my legs rubbery, a tender spot on the bottom of one foot. I had the cane in one hand and the first-aid kit still firmly in the other hand. At least I could fix my foot. I also still had my money, phone and passport all safe in the money belt. I just didn't have my clothes or my hiking boots or my coat or my iPod. Or anything else I needed to climb the mountain.

EIGHT

I stumbled along the street, limping and barefoot. My breath was still strained and I was sweating. People were staring at me—not just the locals but other tourists. How many of them had seen me chasing after my bags only to come back empty-handed? Well, practically empty-handed. I still had the most important thing—the cane—but nobody but me knew how important it was. I wanted to raise it above my head like a trophy. Instead I slinked away, feeling embarrassed and ashamed. I'd been ripped off by a couple of street kids, and I hadn't been smart enough or strong enough or fast enough to stop it from happening. Less than two hours in the country and I'd been arrested and then had all my things stolen. Great start, really in charge.

Up ahead I saw one of my sandals—the left one. I slipped it on. The cut on the bottom of my foot hurt as it hit against the sole, but at least it was a little protection. Who knew what sort of germs would be on the ground here? I scanned the ground for the other sandal; it couldn't be far, but it was nowhere to be seen. I limped along, hoping to find it.

I still had to get to East Africa Walking Tours. Had I passed it in my mad dash or was it farther along? Was I walking in the wrong direction? I stopped. I needed to get my bearings and catch my breath. Why was I still finding it so hard to breathe? I'd been running, and it was hot and humid, but I shouldn't be huffing and puffing like an old man. I was in great shape, but it sure didn't feel like it.

"Excuse me," I called out to two tourists. "Do you know where East Africa Walking Tours is?"

They looked at me, puzzled, and said a few words in what sounded like German.

"It is that way," said a voice behind me.

I turned around. An old man—a local—was pointing up the road. In his other hand was my other sandal!

I limped over, and he handed it to me.

"Thank you."

"Your foot is hurt?"

"It's not that bad," I said. "It's just a scratch."

"Scratches get infected. Take care of it the way you took care of that little boy."

"You saw that?"

He nodded. "That was kind of you," he said. "I saw *everything*. I am so sorry. If I was younger, I would have run down one of those boys for you and got back your bags."

"They were very fast."

"We are a people of runners. But please do not judge us by a few thieves. We are also a people of honor."

I hadn't seen much of that honor. No one had tried to stop them.

"It happened quickly or other people would have done something," he explained.

"It did happen pretty fast. The only one I really saw was the little boy I helped. He's the only one I can identify. At least I think I can."

"If nothing else, you could identify him by the bandage. He will probably be so proud of it that he will not take it off for weeks," the old man said.

"Then I could tell the police to look for the bandage," I suggested.

"I do not believe the little boy was part of it."

"You mean he just fell down and then by coincidence the others were there to take my things?"

"Not coincidence. You were being watched and followed. They were waiting for you to let down your guard and then put down your bags."

"That was just stupid of me," I said. "I should have been more careful."

"You were being careful, not of yourself but of the boy. You were not stupid but kind."

"I won't do that again."

"You won't help someone who needs help?" he asked.

For a split second I almost blurted out "no," but I thought better. My grandpa helped anybody who needed help. "I'd help, but I'd be more careful."

"Good. It is one thing that they stole your possessions. It would be a far worse thing if they were to steal your compassion. Now you need people to help you.

I heard you ask for East Africa Walking Tours. Is that where you wish to go?"

"Yes, please."

"It's not far, but not easy to see. I will show you."

"That's okay, no problem, I can find it."

"It is not a problem. I will show you," he said.

He reached out and took my hand. I was slightly thrown but didn't resist. I'd already noticed local men walking hand in hand, talking.

"You are here to try to climb the mountain?"

"Not to *try*. To *succeed*," I said.

He laughed. "Ah, to be so young and confident."

"I *am* confident."

"Confidence in oneself is a good thing," he said.

"That's what I've always believed," I said, although I knew a couple of my ex-girlfriends, a whole lot of people I'd competed against and a brother who would have said I was more arrogant than confident.

"But you must be careful not to underestimate the mountain," he warned.

"I'm not underestimating it, but like Henry Ford said: 'If you think you can do it, you're probably right, and if you think you can't do it, you're still probably right.'"

"This Henry Ford seems like a very wise man. Did he climb Kilimanjaro?"

"No, he made cars—Fords. He practically invented modern manufacturing."

"Those cars I know. If you could drive to the top of the mountain, I am certain that this Mr. Ford would be correct. As it is, of every ten people who set off on the climb, only six reach the summit."

"I'll be one of those six. I'm young and I'm fit."

"Strangely, it is the young men who fail the most. They do not understand *polepole*."

"I guess I don't understand it either. Po-lee po-lee?"

"It is Swahili for slowly. It is important to move slowly," he explained.

"Where I come from, it's more important to move quickly."

"Ah, but you are *not* where you come from; you are *here*."

My whole plan was to move as quickly as possible. In, up, down, out.

"I can beat the mountain," I said.

"Oh, no, that is not possible," he said, shaking his head vigorously. "You may summit, but you cannot defeat a mountain. You should not even use such words. You do not wish to get the mountain angry."

"Angry? It's a mountain."

"It is more than just a mountain. It is alive."

Just what I needed—a superstitious old man holding my hand and leading me around.

"Beneath those rocks its heart still beats," he continued. "Its blood still flows. If the wind is right, you can smell it breathing." He pulled me to a stop. "Can you smell it?"

Great. Superstitious *and* crazy. Probably believed some African myth about Kilimanjaro being a person or an animal or a spirit. I hoped he'd spare me the story. I didn't like stories unless they were about real things or places and hopefully involved science or math.

"Take a deep breath...smell," he ordered.

I wanted him to let go of my hand and leave me alone, but out of respect I did what I was told and took a deep breath.

"I don't smell anything. Wait...sulfur...I smell sulfur."

"Yes," he said. "Kilimanjaro is a dormant volcano, but not extinct. You can smell the fire beneath the surface. It can still shudder and send down rocks. The glaciers can still crack and roll down the trails."

"Oh, I understand," I said. "I thought you were talking about the mountain having a spirit or something."

"*Everything* has a spirit, and that is why you should be careful what you say. Do not make the mountain angry. I have seen it angry."

"Maybe we better get walking," I suggested, trying to change the subject.

We started again, my hand still in his.

"Have you ever climbed the mountain?" I asked.

"I am an old man. It has been more than a decade since I climbed it the last time and almost seventy years since the first time."

"So you've climbed it a couple of times."

"The first time I was a boy of eleven and the last time I was more than sixty, but yes, I have climbed it more than twice."

"How many times?"

"I did not always count." He shrugged. "Five or six hundred times."

"You mean *five* or *six* times, right?"

He shook his head. "I have climbed it five times in one month."

"What?"

"No, that would not be right...the most in one month would be four."

"Then you really have climbed it hundreds of times?" I gasped.

"Hundreds, but maybe only five hundred. I did not keep track and not every time did I go as far as the summit."

I was now officially back to thinking that he was either crazy or a liar. "It's hard to believe anybody could go up that many times."

"Each year for more than forty years I brought people to the top, first as a porter, then as a guide, until I became too old. In the end, the mountain wore me down and it remains tall." He paused. "Although I believe my steps wore it down just a little. Wore it down, but did not defeat it. We are here." He released my hand.

I saw a little wooden sign—*East Africa Walking Tours.* I might have missed that without his assistance.

"Thanks for helping me find it."

"It is my pleasure. I cannot help people to the top anymore, but today I was still a good guide. I helped in a little way for you to make the climb. They will take care of you now. They are good people and good guides. And promise me you will remember: *polepole*."

"I'll remember," I said. Remembering didn't mean I'd do it.

"And one more thing," he said. "Those boys who stole your things did not do it out of greed, but out of need. It does not make it right, but somehow it makes it less wrong."

NINE

I opened the door and it tripped a bell hanging over the top. The office was dimly lit, and the air was hot and stale. There were a few desks, a table and some bamboo chairs, but no people.

"Hello!" I called out.

There was a commotion from the back, and a girl who looked to be twelve or thirteen poked her head out.

"*Jambo*," she called out, flashing a big smile.

"*Jambo*. I am—"

"You are DJ. My grandfather said you would be coming."

"Is Judge Elijah your grandfather?"

"Yes, he is my father's father. He is a *very* important man. He told us that your grandfather was very important too, and because of that we are to treat you very well."

I wished those street kids had known about that.

"I am Sarah."

"Pleased to meet you."

"I am to take you to your hotel," she said, looking puzzled. "Where are your bags?"

"This is all I've got," I said, holding up the cane and the first-aid kit.

"But you must have more."

"I do. I *did*. My stuff was stolen."

"By who?"

"They didn't stop to introduce themselves. They were kids, about your age. And they got all of my things except this cane, my money and my passport."

"At least they did not take what cannot easily be replaced," Sarah said.

"Can your father help me get new things?"

"We have many things. We have winter coats and hats, which you will need for the top of the mountain," she said, waving to the surrounding shelves that were filled with clothing. "We even have some hiking boots and—" She looked down at my feet. "Your feet, they are *too* big."

"They're size thirteen, but they aren't *too* big."

"No, no," she said, shaking her head. "They *are* much too big. We have no boots that are that big. None!"

"I guess I'll have to buy them at one of the local stores."

"No, not just us, but the stores in the town. There are no boots in all of *Tanzania* that would be that big!"

"Come on, there has to be somewhere that I can—"

"No place! Only elephants in Tanzania have such big feet! Look at your feet and look at my feet!" she said as she gestured to her feet. "Your feet are too big. There are no boots here to fit you."

"Then I'm going to have to go up in these," I said.

"Not possible. You cannot climb in those. No *mzungu* could do that. What about the snow and storms at the top? Your feet would freeze and you would lose your toes. You must have boots."

"But you just said nobody has boots my size."

"No stores, no places, but there might be a way." She paused. "I know people...those who end up collecting things that belong to tourists."

"Collect? You mean like steal? You know who took my stuff?"

"Possibly, or I could find out."

"And you can get my things back? My hiking boots?"

"Not yours maybe, but from other tourists. No locals have such big feet, but maybe one of the other climbers had big feet, so maybe they have collected a pair of boots that is almost as big as you need."

"Almost isn't what I need," I said.

"Almost is better than what you are wearing. And what happened to your foot?"

I looked down. I hadn't realized that my foot had continued to bleed and now a little stream of blood was running off the edge of one sandal.

"I cut it during the chase to get back my things."

"You need to have that treated."

"I'll do that right after we get my stuff back."

"No. First I will bring you to your hotel and you will take care of your foot."

"I want to go with you, right now, and then I'll take care of the foot."

"Right now, I do not know where to go. These people, they do not have a store, you know. I must ask around to find them. If you are with me, nobody will tell me anything. I must go alone while you stay at the hotel."

"I can't just sit there and do nothing," I protested.

"You will not be doing nothing. You will be making sure that your wound is cared for. We cannot argue. I must look before your things are taken out of town and sold elsewhere. We go."

TEN

I waited on an overstuffed couch on the hotel patio, sipping a soda. I'd taken care of my foot, removing a small piece of glass and then thoroughly disinfecting the cut before wrapping it up as well as I could. Then I'd washed the sandal to remove the stain. My foot felt tender when I put weight on it, but it wasn't really painful.

As I sat there, I listened in on the conversations that swirled around me. Everybody at the hotel, with the exception of the staff, was a tourist. There were lots of languages spoken, but English dominated, so I could make out most of what was being said. Half the people were getting ready to climb the mountain. The other half had already climbed or tried to climb.

I was astonished by which people had made it and which had failed. I expected that the young and fit would be successful and the old and fat would fail, but that turned out to not always be the case. I heard one overweight older man—he had to be in his fifties at least—who smoked while he bragged about reaching the summit. A superfit young guy in his twenties was teased by his buddies because he hadn't made it all the way up. It freaked me out that he didn't look that much different from me. Maybe he'd spent so much time lifting weights that he hadn't done enough cardio.

What also surprised me was the age range of the people at the hotel. Most people were on the younger side, with me being the youngest, but there were a number who were well beyond what I'd consider mountain-climbing age, unless there was a special lane for walkers and wheelchairs. They were probably just there to sightsee or to cheer on younger relatives who were going to the top.

I sat until after eight, after dark, and well after the time Sarah said she'd be back. "Back in an hour" had now become almost three. Didn't anybody in Africa know how many minutes were in an hour? I was always on time. I hated to be late or keep people waiting. Even worse, I really hated it when people kept me waiting. It was so disrespectful. If she couldn't find who she was looking for, she was keeping me from looking for the things I'd need. Even if she was right and no stores stocked size-thirteen boots, I might be able to squeeze into a twelve, or even buy an eleven or ten and cut out the toes so I could use them. I'd always found a way to succeed before, and this wasn't going to be any different.

"Hello, DJ." It was Sarah.

"Did you find some stuff that I can use?"

"Not yet, but I think I *can* get what is needed. I need money," she said.

"How much?"

"Maybe eighty thousand shillings."

I almost reacted emotionally to the number before I did the conversion in my head. That was about $50.

I pulled out the money in my pocket: $60. The rest of my money, along with my passport and the cane, was locked in the hotel safe. I wasn't going to risk losing those things as well.

Sarah took the money from me.

"I will be back in less than an hour," she said.

"I'm going to go with you."

She shook her head vigorously. "No, no, it would not be safe for you to go."

"Then it's even less safe for you to go without me. There's safety in numbers."

"I do not think it would be wise for you to come."

"I don't see a choice. I need to be there at least to try on the hiking boots," I said, grasping for a convincing reason.

"I just do not think that—"

"Look." I got to my feet so I towered over her. "It's my money, my things, my hiking boots, and I'm coming along."

"I will not argue, but do not say that I did not warn you."

"This way," Sarah said.

What had seemed smart sitting on the veranda of the hotel quickly seemed less wise as we wove our way through small streets, back alleys and narrow footpaths cutting between huts and shacks. I followed her down another twist in the pathway between the shacks. This new route was even narrower. At times I had to practically turn sideways to pass.

Lining the cramped passages were huts and small shops that were really just stalls thrown together with random pieces of wood, sheets of corrugated metal, cardboard and plastic. The air was stained with smoke, so strong and thick I could almost taste it.

The only light along our route came from a few kerosene lamps hanging from poles or sitting on sills or shining through the small openings of the buildings. Outside of these faint leaks of light, the darkness completely engulfed everything.

The darkness was both reassuring and unnerving. I couldn't see very well, but at least *I* was less visible. It felt like my white skin could almost go unnoticed. Of course that was just wishful thinking.

When any light did catch me, it felt as if my skin practically glowed as the light reflected off its whiteness. There was no hiding. I could tell by the reaction I was getting as I followed Sarah. People's eyes widened in surprise and there was a ripple of conversation that grew louder as we passed. I could hear the unmistakable word *mzungu.*

A procession of little children trailed behind me. When I turned around, they stopped in their tracks, bumping into each other or even starting to scatter, but as soon as I started walking they rejoined the procession. It made me realize that having a white guy here, particularly at night, was a big source of amusement and entertainment. Hopefully I wasn't going to be part of anything more exciting, although I was becoming increasingly more anxious.

Occasionally the way would open up onto clearings filled with pecking chickens and lots of children. Some of the kids were sitting on the ground, and some were kicking around a ball that was nothing more than tightly wrapped pieces of plastic held together with rope or string. We passed by a number of identical-looking dogs, so similar in appearance that I thought at first it was the same dog—

skinny and brown and cowering—acting as if it expected me to kick it.

Then Sarah would lead me into another passageway. Did she really know where we were going? At least if we did get lost, there were lots of people to ask for directions. Aside from our little entourage, there was a constant stream of people walking along in both directions and even more peering out from darkened doorways and windows as we passed. It seemed like every eye was on us—on *me*. I was glad that the rest of my valuables were all locked up, although it would have been nice to have the cane to use as a weapon if I needed it.

I was feeling increasingly claustrophobic. It was a combination of the darkness, the smoke and the scale of everything. Relatively speaking I was *gigantic*. And strangely, it felt as if I was actually getting *bigger* as we walked, like Gulliver in the land of Lilliput. Being bigger should have been better, but it just made me feel more visible. Besides, I remembered what those Lilliputians did to Gulliver when they tied him down to the ground.

I kept one eye on Sarah while my head swiveled back and forth trying to watch all around me as they all seemed to watch me. She stopped and I practically bumped into her, and a couple of members of my entourage bumped into me. I looked down, and their eyes widened in shock as they scampered away, knocking down a few others, who in turn started to run as well, causing a little ripple of running kids. In spite of everything—or maybe because of it—I burst out laughing and my voice filled the air.

"In here," Sarah said, pointing to a small hut.

She pushed open the door and disappeared inside. I hesitated for a few seconds before I ducked down and stepped into the darkness. I looked around, letting my eyes adjust.

"Over here," Sarah called out.

I saw her shadowy outline and followed. We went through the back of the hut and entered a dimly lit courtyard. Sarah shook hands with a boy who looked about my age but smaller. They exchanged a rapid burst of conversation, and I was pretty sure that I was the subject of that discussion. The boy looked nervous, his eyes shifting anxiously, and I was afraid he was about to bolt.

Finally the voices became quieter and calmer, and he came over with Sarah. I looked into his eyes and he looked away, but in that brief connection I just knew he wasn't somebody who could be trusted.

He turned and Sarah followed. I settled in behind. We left the courtyard through an opening in the fence, went down yet another little passageway, and then I skidded to a stop. We were standing in a little market square, much more brightly lit, and in front of me was a stall, its shelves filled with merchandise. Two more people, about the same age as our guide, were standing in front of the stall.

I scanned the length of the stall. There were T-shirts, skirts, toys, shoes, hammers and screwdrivers, suitcases and some backpacks—including mine. I had to fight the urge to yell something out or rush over to reclaim it. A little farther along was my other bag, and there were my hiking boots! My stuff was here. Were these the kids who had ripped me off? I looked closely at their faces as they talked, trying to see if they had been the ones. But really, all that I'd seen was the backs of their heads. Maybe I could ask them to turn around. Okay, that was stupid.

Sarah and the first boy spoke to the other two, who also seemed to be perturbed, probably upset about my being here. They exchanged anxious bursts of conversation and shot nervous glances in my direction. It gave me a strange sort of satisfaction that I was at least causing them some distress. If they tried to leave, I was still going to grab my boots and my bag and whatever else of mine I could find.

Sarah returned from speaking to the boys. "They say that they would be *most* pleased to sell you some merchandise."

"They want to sell me my own stuff," I hissed. "How big of them."

"Yes, they will sell to you if you meet their price."

"Their price? Those are *my* things! The things that were—"

"Keep your voice down. Do not get them excited."

"I don't care if they're excited."

"Oh, you *should* care, very much. We want everything to be friendly."

"You want me to be friends with the people who ripped me off?" I asked quietly.

"I want you to be friendly with them, not become friends. We want to remain friendly while you purchase back the items you need."

"I can't believe you want me to buy back my own things."

"They *were* your things. Now they are *their* things."

"But that's not right," I protested.

Sarah turned around to face the three boys. "He is just deciding what things he wishes to purchase," she called out. "He says you have very fine merchandise!"

The three boys nodded and waved and smiled.

She turned back toward me. "It does not matter if it is right or wrong, this is what must be done."

"Look, what if I just grabbed my stuff? They couldn't stop us. I'm bigger than all of them combined, and there are two of us and only three of them."

"There are only three that you can *see*," she said. "All around are many, many more members of their street families. Besides, if there was to be a fight, there are not two of us; there is only you."

"I know you're just a girl, but still you could—"

"Oh, no, you don't understand," she said, cutting me off. "If there is a fight, I would join them. Never is it wise to be on the side of a crazy person, and you would be crazy to risk our lives for a few shillings."

"But what about the *principle* of the thing? You're asking me to buy my *own* things."

"As I said, your things now belong to these people. You have the money to buy them, so just buy them so we can leave," she whispered. "Be grateful that you can have your things back."

"What if we went and got the police to come and arrest them?" I suggested.

"You do not understand. The minute we go they will leave, and along with them would go your things, never to be seen again. And even if you could find the police they would not come with you tonight. You have to understand that the police do not like to come in here at night. They think it is *too* dangerous."

It suddenly dawned on me where I was and what we were doing. I wasn't standing in line at Walmart. I was in a place that was too dangerous for the police to come.

"Okay, fine. Let's go *shopping* for my things."

I went to the first stall and picked up my pack, which was going to hold my things on the climb to the top of the mountain. Now it would hold the things I needed to reclaim. I sifted through some more items. There were my cargo pants and five pairs of socks—two of them special "toe" socks designed to keep each toe separate and cushioned—and my shirts and running shoes and of course my hiking boots. Item by item I put them into the pack until I came to the boots. I went to put them into the pack and one of the boys stepped forward and stopped me, saying something I didn't understand.

"He wants for you to try them on to make sure they fit," Sarah explained.

"Oh, I'm pretty sure they'll fit unless my feet have changed sizes in the last few hours."

"Just do as he asks," Sarah said.

Almost instantly one of the other boys materialized holding a little three-legged stool. I sat down and pulled a pair of socks—my socks—out of the pack. I kicked off the sandals, pulled on the socks and then slipped my foot into one of the boots.

The same boy said something and Sarah translated. "He wants to know if they fit."

"Tell him they are too small and I want to know if he has something bigger."

Sarah looked shocked.

"Go ahead and tell him."

Sarah gave me a sly smile and then spoke. The boy looked as surprised as she had.

"Ask him if he has any bigger ones because I do not really like these much."

Sarah translated and the boy replied.

"He says there are no bigger ones in Tanzania, and he thought for sure they would fit you as if they were your own."

"Tell him they are too small and too ugly, but I will take them if the price is right."

Sarah burst into laughter and then told the boy, who also started to laugh. He slapped her on the back.

"He says the price will be good because he likes you. He says you are a good *mzungu*."

I did up the laces on the boots, making sure they were tied tightly. I wasn't giving back these boots and I wanted to have something better than sandals if I had to run.

I searched the stall again until I was certain that I'd located all of my things. What I couldn't fit into my pack I put into my other bag—the green duffel bag. I did a rough tally in my head, trying to remember what else was missing, what else I still had to find. I basically had everything I could think of, including my special flashlight—the one I would wear on my head like a mining light.

"That's it," I said.

"Good. We will negotiate a price."

The two of them began talking. The conversation quickly became excited, and I could tell that they had very different ideas about what I should pay. I wished I could have been part of the discussion or at least understood what they were saying. The one boy turned away and joined the other two, and the three of them began an equally noisy discussion.

"I have offered them around twenty thousand shillings," Sarah said to me.

"But you told me to bring—"

"Be quiet. Do not let them hear the number. Numbers in English they understand. We are negotiating. They wish to have one hundred and fifty thousand shillings!"

"I don't have that much money with me!"

"And we will not pay that much. This is how things are done here. I will talk them down."

Sarah turned to the boys and yelled out something, and instantly all three of them burst into laughter, one of them laughing so hard that he almost fell over.

"What did you say to them?" I asked.

"I told them that if they didn't sell the boots to you that they would have to hope that an elephant needed footwear or perhaps a small family could use one of them as a hut."

The first boy returned, and he and Sarah again started talking, throwing sentences back and forth. Finally, judging from the nodding of heads, I thought they'd reached a decision.

"Give me your money," Sarah said. "And turn your pockets inside out so they can see that you carry nothing more."

I did what I was told.

There were more arguments, more discussion, and then finally Sarah gave them the money. The boy looked at me and said something.

"He is telling you that it was a pleasure to do business with you and that he hopes you always keep an eye on your things."

"Tell him he's a no good—"

"I will pass on your thanks and appreciation," Sarah said.

They exchanged a few more words; she shook hands with the boy, who then shook my hand, and the three of them turned and vanished into the darkness.

"What about the rest of their things?" I asked, gesturing to the still-full market stall.

"These things are not theirs—only the things that they stole from you belonged to them and now, once again, belong to you. We must leave and leave quickly."

I didn't need a second invitation. We left the little market square and headed in the opposite direction from the boys. Waiting at the exit was my entourage of children, which seemed to be much larger now. They scattered like a flock of birds, trying to get out of our way. No sooner had we passed than they fell in behind us. Sarah was moving fast, and I found myself out of breath trying to keep up with her. At least now we were moving in the right direction. Things were getting bigger—the pathway, the buildings, and the spaces between the buildings—and we burst onto a street, a real street with real shops. There were some other tourists strolling down the street. We were safe! I let out a big sigh of relief.

Sarah slowed down and I came up beside her.

"That was a little scary," I said.

"If you were not *very* scared, you did not understand what we just did."

"I guess I didn't really understand, but at least it all ended well. But it almost didn't, right? He wanted more money than I had, didn't he?"

"Yes, he demanded more, but I made a deal. I said to him that if he somehow is *mistakenly* arrested as a thief and taken before a judge, that he could mention my name, the *granddaughter* of Elijah, and I would come and testify that he was of good character and he would be released."

"And would you do that?"

"I gave my word."

"Thanks for doing all of that. I really do owe you one."

"Part of how you can pay me back is to not mention any of this to anybody, especially my father. He would think poorly of you for losing your things," she explained.

There was something about her expression that made me think that there was more that she wasn't saying. And then it came to me.

"You also don't want anyone to know *how* I got my things back, do you?"

She shook her head. "We would both be in trouble, but especially me. What we did was not so wise."

I wondered just how "not so wise" it had been.

"There is one thing that you could do to repay me," she said.

"Just name it."

"I want you to tell my father that you want me to be one of your porters when you climb the mountain."

"Sure, of course, that's no problem."

"I will tell him that you wish to have somebody your age along," she said.

"How old are you?" I asked, sure that she wasn't *my* age.

"I am fifteen."

"I'm almost eighteen, so we're not exactly the same age."

"Not the same, but I am closer to you than others. So I will tell him that you insisted on me coming along."

"Sure, you can tell him that I want you to come," I said.

"Not just want—*insist*. I will tell him it is a special request from the grandson of his father's good friend. Then he will not be able to say no."

"Okay, tell him I insist that I won't climb the mountain without you. I really do owe you this."

"Thank you."

"And what happened tonight will be our secret."

"Good, a secret. Now I will get you back to the hotel. Tomorrow you will meet my father and the members of your climbing group, and the details of the climb will be discussed."

I wondered if I'd already seen the rest of my group. There were so many people at the hotel, it was hard to tell.

"For each member of the party there will be two porters. With any luck I will be one of your porters. We will carry your things."

"I agreed you could come along, but I can carry my own things," I said. I was so much bigger than Sarah that I could have carried *her*.

"You will carry your clothes, but we will carry water and food, the tent and sleeping bag," she explained.

"When we go camping at home, I always carry all of my own things," I said.

"You have climbed a mountain when you camped before?" she asked.

"Not a mountain, but I've done a lot of camping and a lot of hiking at the lake we go to."

"This is no lake. You cannot reach the top without porters. It is not legal to climb without them and a guide. Those are the rules."

The rules were probably there to insure that people got work. There was no point in arguing.

"Fine, and I insist that you're one of my porters."

"Good. You must keep your word...especially the secret part."

"I give you my word." I paused. "I was just wondering, how hard is it to make the climb?"

"It is harder for some than others," she said, which didn't help me much.

"And is it hard for you?" I asked.

"It has never been hard for *me*."

"So you've always made it to the top."

"I have never failed."

"How many times have you been to the top?"

"Never."

"But you said you never failed."

"The reason I have never failed and that it has not been hard is because I have never climbed the mountain before."

"What?"

"My father says I am still too young and a girl, so he has not let me go up. But now that you insist, he *cannot* argue. Because of you I will climb the mountain for the first time!"

"But, but—"

"Do not try to back out of our agreement!" she snapped. "You have given your word. Does your word mean nothing?"

I was caught. Not only was I getting in the middle of a family fight but one of my porters also had no climbing experience. Maybe I *would* have to carry her up.

"Will you keep your word?" she asked.

I nodded. "I always keep my word."

ELEVEN

I walked into the dining hall. There was a little sign on one of the tables—*Reserved East Africa Walking Tours.* We were supposed to start our meeting in ten minutes, but if this was like most of the meetings and schedules in Africa that might mean two hours from now. Either way, I was on time—which meant I was early.

I slumped into one of the seats, hoping the meeting wouldn't take too long. Sarah had told me that the next morning we would be gathering our things and doing the first stage of the trip: the 20-kilometer drive to the base camp.

Maybe this was a good time to let my mother know that everything was okay. I pulled out my phone and sent her a short text message.

Hey Mom and Steve too. I hope you are doing well. All is good here. Just getting ready to meet and start out. I figure 2 days up and 1 down. Back on the plane soon after and back home in less than 5. Don't worry about me. Everything is perfect–see you soon...and little brother remember if you need help I'm only a text away.

I pushed *Send* and the message left, traveling halfway around the world. Of course they probably wouldn't read it for a while. It was still morning here which meant it was the middle of the night there. It would be a nice little surprise waiting for my mother when she woke up.

My phone signaled I'd gotten a message. I guess my mom was still up. That wasn't a good sign. But it wasn't from my mom—it was from Steve!

That's right, he was already in Spain! We were practically in the same time zone. I opened the message.

Doing my task. If u need any help let ME know.

Regardless, the important thing was that he'd started his adventure. Finishing it might be a different story. He had a track record of starting things and then quitting. That was probably why I was given the task of climbing the mountain. Quitting didn't get you to the top. I was glad he was on his way though. Nothing ever got finished that didn't get started.

An older woman approached the table. She looked familiar—maybe I'd seen her around the hotel. She was either here to go on a safari or was waiting for somebody to get back from a climb.

"Hello, dear, good to see you again," she said. "I'm Doris."

Again? Wait…the accent. She was the woman from the customs lineup. "Pleased to see you again too," I said as we shook hands. "I'm DJ."

She sat down, probably tired from the walk across the dining hall. I figured there was no harm in her being here until my group got here.

"You must be very excited about the climb," she said.

"Very excited."

"I must admit that I'm a little nervous," she said.

Why would she be nervous? Was she waiting for someone to come back from the climb?

"There's nothing to be worried about."

"I'm sure you're right," she said. "But I've read that over thirty percent of the people who start the climb don't make it to the top."

"I've read that too."

"And they say that at least ten people a year die during the climb," she added.

That I hadn't heard. That made *me* a little nervous. I tried to reassure her. "I'm sure that whoever you're waiting for will be fine."

"I'm not waiting for anybody. I'm here to climb the mountain."

"You?" I exclaimed. "But you're old." I corrected myself. "I mean, *older*...than most people."

She laughed. I was glad I hadn't offended her.

"The oldest person to successfully complete the climb was eighty-one," she said. "And in case you're wondering, I'm not that old. I'm only sixty-seven."

I wasn't sure how to respond. I didn't see much difference between old and really old. Besides, that guy in his eighties must have been like a super athlete. She didn't look like that.

I looked up to see Sarah and the man I assumed was her father coming toward us. She smiled and waved. He didn't do either. In fact, he was scowling.

"This is my father," Sarah said.

I got up. "Pleased to meet you, sir," I said, extending my hand.

He took it and shook it, gripping it hard—really hard. That scowl hardened before he finally released my hand.

"And this must be Doris," he said. He smiled at her and they shook hands. "My name is Elijah Odogo."

"Most pleased to meet you, Mr. Odogo," she said.

"Please, please, it is Elijah."

He looked at his watch. "It is time to begin. It is unfortunate that the remaining members of our party are not here. I do not like to be late."

That must have made him one of the few people in Africa who thought that way. Despite the scowl, I liked that he wanted to start on time.

"I have asked my daughter to come to the briefing as she will be accompanying us on this journey."

"How nice it must be for you to have your daughter come with us," Doris said.

"Yes, nice," he said, but neither his tone nor expression matched his words. "We will begin our briefing without the missing members. If they have not arrived at the agreed-upon time tomorrow morning, they will not make the climb either."

He sat down, as did Sarah. She looked very subdued.

"I am most pleased to be your guide up the mountain," he began. "Each climber will be accompanied by two porters. The porters are very experienced and have all made many, many summits of the mountain...well, with the one exception." He glanced at Sarah and then looked at me and scowled again. "We have an *excellent* record. Our summit rate is almost eighty percent."

That did sound good.

"We will be taking the Machame route. From the start to the summit, it is just over forty-one kilometers."

That didn't sound so bad. Less than a marathon. Last year I'd run a marathon in less than five hours.

"Of course it is not the distance but the climb. The summit is five thousand meters above where we now sit. The elevation change is what presents the greatest challenge. You can expect that you will experience symptoms of mountain sickness to varying degrees," he said.

"What are the symptoms?" Doris asked.

"Headaches, shortness of breath, nausea and general fatigue mark the initial stages of mountain sickness," I said.

Elijah looked at me, eyebrows raised.

"I read about it online, although those symptoms don't sound that bad to me," I explained. "Who hasn't had a headache before?"

"A headache yes, mountain sickness, no," he said.

From his look I knew that I should probably shut up.

"Moderate mountain sickness involves a headache that does not respond to medication. Shortness of breath continues even when sitting or lying down. Nausea becomes vomiting, and fatigue causes the hiker to feel as if he can no longer move forward."

"That doesn't sound very pleasant," Doris said.

"Not pleasant. Acute symptoms involve a headache so severe that it feels as if the head is about to explode, slurred speech, blueness of the lips and face, gurgling in the chest as liquid builds in the lungs. Sometimes climbers fall into unconsciousness."

"Does that happen very often?" I asked anxiously.

"It happens."

"And what do you do when it happens?" Doris asked.

"The person is rushed down the mountain, carried on a stretcher by the porters as quickly as possible."

"And if they weren't brought right down?" I asked.

"They would die," he said. "But that is rare. There are less than fifteen deaths every year."

"I thought it was only ten," I said.

"Are you questioning my knowledge?" he asked, staring right at me.

"No, sir, I just read that—"

"Do you believe you are the guide?" he scoffed.

"No, sir. Sorry, sir," I said, breaking away from his stare and looking down.

"Have you had to bring people down by stretcher?" Doris asked.

"Many times."

"And deaths?" she asked.

He held up one finger. "Only one and that was many years ago."

"Was it mountain sickness?" I asked.

He nodded. "Most unfortunate. But I will watch you all. We will walk together. Nobody will die, but some will not make the summit."

I knew he was talking about Doris. Maybe it was even better that she was so old because she'd probably have to quit quickly and wouldn't slow us down for long.

"You will each provide three kilograms of personal gear for each of your porters to carry," he said.

"That's all they carry?" I blurted out. It didn't seem like much.

"They also carry your sleeping bags, tents, food and cooking utensils," he said. "Which is why each porter must be not only young but strong." He paused and I had a feeling I knew what he was going to say next. "Unfortunately some porters may be too young and not strong enough…we will see."

"Are there limits to how much we carry?" I asked, thinking that ultimately I might be carrying at least some of the things that Sarah was supposed to carry.

"You may carry two hundred kilograms if you wish," he said. "At least, if you wish never to reach the top."

"How much should we carry?" Doris asked.

"I would recommend no more than five kilograms."

"But what if we're bigger?" I asked.

"Bigger is not necessarily better," he said. "You are already carrying much more than anybody else. You are very, very big."

"I'm a football player," I said.

"You do not look like a football player," he said.

"No, not soccer, football—American football. I'm a linebacker."

"Here your extra weight, be it fat or muscle, is simply more weight. Hopefully you will not slow us down too much," he said.

I wanted to say something in response to his attack on me, but I was smart enough to keep my mouth shut.

"Do you know that those who fail to make the climb are most often young men in their twenties?" he said.

"I didn't know that," Doris said. "Why would that be?"

"They have much muscle here," he said, flexing his arm, "and little muscle up here." He placed a finger against his head. "They go too fast, they do not listen... they act like they know more than the guide."

That last part—okay, maybe the whole part—was obviously aimed at me. I wanted to argue or disagree, but that would have proven his point. I didn't need to tell him; I'd show him. He'd just given me a little more incentive.

"There is no shame in not reaching the top," he said.

That was meant for Doris.

"We will be flexible in our climb to better ensure our chances of reaching the summit. I will not rule out a sixth or seventh day if necessary, but we will try for five days."

"What?" I questioned. "You think it'll take five days?"

"But possibly seven. Do you think you will need more?"

"Of course not! I was thinking maybe two or three days would do it."

He laughed. "You were not thinking at all. Only a Chagga guide could make the summit and return in two days."

"I said maybe two or three."

"It is not possible. Do you wish to reach the summit?" he demanded.

"That's what I came here to do."

"That attitude is what makes young men fail. I cannot let you fail. I have given my word. You must listen and do as you are told. Understood?"

Reluctantly I nodded my head. What choice did I have? It wasn't like I could make the climb without him...or could I? Of course not.

"Remember, reaching the top is always optional. Coming back down is mandatory." He got to his feet. "We will meet tomorrow morning in the lobby at six. I wish you a good sleep and good luck, because you will need both to reach the summit." He paused and looked directly at me. "That and a good dose of humility."

I nodded and then turned to walk back to my hotel to sleep and eat.

TWELVE

The truck twisted and turned, bumped and snaked, roared and fumed as it climbed up the dirt road that led to the start of the trek. Doris was up front with the driver and Elijah. Sarah and all the other porters had already gone ahead. Apparently they walked this section that we drove. In the back with me were the other three members of our party. They hadn't just missed the pre-climb meeting, they'd almost missed the whole trip. Judging from the smell of alcohol that was coming off them and the fact that they'd either gone to sleep or passed out almost the instant they got in the truck, they'd probably been out partying all night.

In the few minutes they were awake, it was obvious that they wouldn't have been much for conversation with me even if they were conscious. One of them spoke a little bit of English and the other two spoke none whatsoever. All I knew was their names—Tomas, Joki and Kaarl—and that they were Finnish. They were young and looked fit enough to be professional athletes. I figured there'd be four of us who made the summit. At least assuming that there were no bars on the way up the mountain.

Between the fumes—diesel from the engine of the truck and alcohol from my fellow passengers—and the bumps and swerves of the ride, I was starting to wonder if I could keep my breakfast down. Maybe it would have been better to walk instead of ride this section. If the porters could do it, I could do it.

The truck came to a stop and the diesel fumes subsided. With one hand on the side rail, I got up just as Mr. Odogo appeared and lowered the truck's tailgate.

"We are here," he said.

I grabbed my pack and jumped down as the other three woke up. Mr. Odogo started to talk to them and I walked away, around the side of the truck, and there it was: the mountain. It filled the entire horizon. It took my breath away. Brilliant green forest filled the foreground, giving way to the grays and browns and black rock, finally topped by white—the snows of Kilimanjaro.

It was so big and so tall that as I stood there looking at it, I wondered for the first time, Can I do this? Can I do what Grandpa asked me to do? I swallowed those questions. There was no room for doubt. I turned away from the mountain. I had one more thing to do before I started.

I walked away until I was by myself and then pulled the second letter out of my pocket. I was at the bottom of the mountain. It was time. I felt a sense of anticipation, wondering what he'd written. I started to open it and then stopped. I really did want to read it, but I realized that after this one there was only one more letter to read—one more private moment to share with him.

I took a deep breath and pulled the letter out.

Hello DJ,

You must be looking at the mountain. The first time I saw the mountain I was young—not as young as you, but certainly a young man. After all that I'd seen and lived through during the war, I didn't think anything could inspire such awe in me. I couldn't believe anything could be that massive and beautiful and peaceful. It stood there silently. The gleaming white top descended to grays and blacks, finally swallowed by the forest at its feet.

At almost 6,000 meters it is the tallest mountain on the continent, the roof of Africa, the highest freestanding mountain in the world. The name Kilimanjaro comes from two Swahili words—kilima, which means hill, and njaro, which means white or shining, for the snow on its peak. The local people, the Chagga, claim that when you stand at the summit you are between heaven and earth. I know all the facts. I just never made the summit. I swore that I would, but somehow life got in the way. There was never time when I was there because there seemed to be so much time, and then I left so suddenly and never had an opportunity to return. I used to tell myself that I had flown over it so many times that it was as if I'd climbed above it. That was nothing more than a not very clever way of rationalizing my failure. Today you set out on a mission to finally bring me to the top.

I can only imagine what you must be feeling. I think I know what I would be feeling—excitement, anticipation and a healthy dose of fear and doubt. Can I make it to the top? Will the mountain defeat me or will I manage to subdue it long enough to reach the summit? For you those thoughts may not exist or they may be even stronger. Don't let the weight of my ashes—the weight of my last request—be too heavy for you to shoulder. You have to know that while my request is that you take my ashes to the summit, all I really need is for you to try. You have succeeded by simply trying. That's all I can ask of you. Not that I don't hope that you will reach the top. Not for me, but for you.

There is a saying—if you wish to travel fast, travel alone; if you wish to travel far, travel together. You are part of a group of climbers, supported by porters and led by a guide. Travel with them. That's important for the climb and in life. Don't leave people behind—not your mother, not your brother, not your cousins—on your life journey.

As you trek up the mountain, I want you to stop along the way, enjoy each step, each moment. Breathe in the air, savor the view, live in the moment. Move slowly, enjoy. Remember not to wish away the minute or the days between now and the goal you are seeking. When you look up, you'll see climbers farther along the journey.

When you look back you'll see those behind you. Don't pity those below or envy those above. Life is a journey and not a destination; each must take it at his own pace. I'm so happy to be sharing this last journey with you.

And most important, remember how much I love you.

Grandpa.

"Thanks, Grandpa," I said under my breath. "And don't worry, I'll get you to the top."

I folded the letter and carefully placed it back in the envelope and then put the envelope into my pack, right between the letter I'd already opened and the one that remained. It was time to try.

THIRTEEN

Sarah and the other porters were dividing up the things they were going to be carrying. She was *so* different from all the other porters. Not just female and younger, but smaller. If only I'd known what her request meant, I would never have agreed. Aside from the flack from Mr. Odogo, could she actually do this?

I walked over and watched the porters talk. Really, *talk* wasn't the right word. They were arguing. I thought they were fighting about who should carry what and Sarah was at the center of the argument. She seemed to be giving as good as she was getting.

Finally the arguing stopped. Sarah and the other porters gathered up their things and packed their duffels and lifted up their loads.

My second porter—I wish I could remember his name—lifted a gigantic load onto his back.

"Thanks for helping to carry my things," I said to him.

He grunted, turned away and started up the hill, joining the line of porters.

"I guess he doesn't understand English," I said to Sarah.

"He understands you. He just doesn't like you."

"Why doesn't he like me?"

"None of the porters like you."

"But...but...why not? Did I do something to offend them?"

"Oh, yes, very much. They are *very* offended."

"Tell them I didn't mean to offend them. I'm really sorry and I'll try to fix what I did wrong!"

"I know that you did not mean to offend them, but you cannot fix it now. It is done. You gave me your word."

"You mean that this is all because I insisted that you come along?"

She nodded. "It is stupid but true. They do not like that I am the first female porter to climb the mountain."

"You're joking, right?"

"No. The first and the youngest as well. Usually even males do not become porters until they reach at least sixteen years of age."

"I didn't know that!" I protested. "I knew it was your first time, but I didn't know you were the first female."

"If I had told you, then you might not have agreed."

"You tricked me."

"I did no trick," she said. "It is not my fault that you know so little."

"Just tell them it isn't really my fault—it's *yours*. They should be mad at *you*."

"They *are* mad at me. Nobody will be talking to me on this climb either. They hope I will fail. They hope we *both* fail."

"That's just stupid, especially the part about you being female and not being able to do the job. Where I come from, there's no difference between males and females."

She gave me a questioning look. "That must be very difficult...if there is no difference between males and females, how do you have babies?"

I felt myself blush. "No, we're different...you know...we have different parts," I stammered. "I just mean we're the same."

"Do you mean that your females are as big as you?" she exclaimed.

"No, no, not as big. I'm bigger than any female I know. It's just...maybe I'm not explaining this very well."

"You are definitely not explaining it well. What do you mean?" she asked.

"I mean we're equal...or we're supposed to be equal. Women are as smart and capable as men."

"Oh, those poor women, that is *so* sad for them."

"Why is that sad?"

"Here, women are *much* smarter than men. It is sad that your women are only equal to men."

"Very funny."

"Not funny. It is a *fact*," she said. "Here, women are superior."

"If women are more capable, then why won't they let women be porters?"

"We women usually use our heads and not our backs. I want to show them that I can use both. That is most threatening to them."

"I guess that's why you let them be in charge, so you don't threaten their delicate egos," I said sarcastically.

"That is exactly right. We women are so smart that we let the men *think* that they are the head. We women are the neck. We tell the head in which direction to look."

I must have looked skeptical, because she said, "I do not really expect you to understand. After all, you are merely a male."

"Yeah, right."

"Yes, it is right. Let me try to explain," Sarah said. "A little baby boy and little baby girl are born at the same time. The little girl will roll over first, sit up first, talk first and walk first. Eventually the boy will catch up—at about seventy years of age—and he will be so shocked he will die."

"Do you really expect me to believe that?"

"No, of course not. You are too young. When you are about seventy you will understand. Of course then you will die. Now it is time to climb."

I'd been so distracted that I hadn't noticed that everybody else had started up the slope. Up ahead, the last of our party, Doris, was just making her way along the trail, and as I watched, she disappeared around a bend, hidden by the rainforest.

Sarah hefted the bag onto her shoulder.

"Let me help," I said.

"No!" she said. "You may not help me."

"But you're carrying my stuff."

"I am your porter. I am supposed to carry your things."

"But I could help—"

"You cannot help. For two reasons. If you carried things, then the others would be right—a girl cannot be a porter. I must carry my share of things."

"And the second reason?" I asked.

"You *cannot* carry your own things. You would never make it to the top carrying this much weight."

"Look, Sarah, I'm twice as big as you and probably four times as strong and—"

"And I am Chagga. This is my heritage. This is what my people do. If I fail, or you fail because of me, there may never be female porters on the mountain. Not now and not for a long, long time, maybe never.

I must carry the load and I must make the summit. We both must make the summit."

"We will," I said.

"Me, I am sure of," she said. "You...I do not know. We shall see."

She turned and started up the hill, chasing after our party. I pulled on my backpack and started after her. I wanted to catch up to continue our conversation, but she was moving quickly. I doubled my pace. At least I tried to double my pace. The mud on the ground was thick, and I was sinking in deeply with each step. Sarah, who was carrying more weight on her back but far less on her body, didn't seem to be sinking nearly as deep. It was almost as if she was skimming over the ground while I was plowing through it. With each step I'd sink in and then have to work to pull out my foot as the mud tried to keep me in place. This wasn't easy, and I could feel the strain, not only in my legs but also in my lungs.

Sarah continued to pull away, getting farther ahead of me with each step. I was, however, slowly catching up to Doris. The three Finns were farther ahead, almost out of sight, and moving quickly.

I changed my goal. It didn't look like I was going to be able to catch Sarah, but I should be able to close the gap between me and Doris. Wow, that was my goal...to outwalk a senior citizen. A great way to succeed was to set the bar low enough, but this was aiming pretty low.

The path was a muddy rut, a little reddish-brown ribbon that sliced through the green rainforest that pressed in on both sides. It was so close, so dense, that it was almost suffocating. It felt like the forest was sucking the oxygen out of my lungs, which of course made no sense. Forests *gave* off oxygen. I couldn't help but think about what might be hiding in the forest. Were there really leopards in there? My head started swiveling back and forth, side to side as well as up and down. The forest was now not just pressing in on both sides, but was starting to overhang the trail. If I were a leopard, that's where I'd be, sitting up there, waiting to pounce.

I looked up the trail again. Doris had vanished. She'd gone over a little rise and disappeared. I was alone. If there was a leopard, it would just be me and it. I didn't think I could outfight or outrun it. I wished I had something I could use as a weapon.

I thought about my pack. I guess I could throw a roll of biodegradable toilet paper at it, or hit it with my walking stick. The best thing was not to be alone. I had to catch up to Doris. Not that she could protect me, but I figured that even if I couldn't outrun a leopard, I could outrun a senior citizen.

What a terrible thing to think! I wouldn't really abandon her if we were attacked, but still...being with somebody would make me feel better. I just had to—

There was a crash above my head, and I jumped to the side. It was a little monkey, leaping from one branch to another. It stared down at me. It looked like it was smirking. I was being laughed at by a monkey. I guessed that was better than being dined on by a leopard.

I dug in a little deeper, straining up the little hill and over the top. Doris was there, just in front of me, doubled over! She'd collapsed! I rushed over, only to find her sitting on the ground, camera in hand, taking a picture of one of the little flowers that littered the floor of the forest.

"I love flowers," she said.

"Yeah, they're nice."

"I think as you get older you learn more and more to stop and smell the flowers...and take pictures of them."

"My grandfather loved flowers."

"Loved...past tense," she said. "Your grandfather died?"

"A little while ago."

"And you're here now?" she questioned. Instantly she looked sorry for asking. "I understand. It's hard when plans have been made and it's impossible to rearrange things. I'm sure your grandfather wouldn't have wanted you to miss this."

"I'm here because of him."

"He arranged your trip?" she asked.

"Arranged and financed. It was one of his last requests. He asked me to climb the mountain to..." I stopped myself. I wasn't supposed to tell anybody what I was doing, but it felt like I needed to tell her. "He asked me to scatter his ashes at the top. They're here in his walking stick," I said, turning around slightly so she could see the stick tied to the back of my pack.

"That is such a wonderful thing for you to do!"

She got to her feet, reached up and wrapped her arms around me, pulling me down with such force that I almost tumbled over on top of her. She was shockingly strong. She released me from her grip and I straightened up. She wasn't just old, but small, very small.

"He must have been very special to you."

"He was the best." I felt tears coming to my eyes.

"I'll do anything in my power to help you."

I couldn't help but think that the best thing she could do was to drop out of the climb right now so she wouldn't slow me down.

"I know you're probably asking yourself what an old woman like me can do to help you."

I felt guilty. "No, that wasn't what I was thinking at all," I lied. Hopefully it was a convincing lie.

"I'll be with you every step of the way," she said.

"Thanks, and I'll be there for you," I said. Why did I say that?

"That is so sweet," she said. "I guess we better get climbing again. The summit isn't coming to us. We just have to remember to go *polepole.*"

"Yeah, slowly," I muttered.

"That comes a little more naturally at my age, but remember that slow and steady wins the race."

I smiled at her and nodded, although I really didn't agree at all. Moving slowly had never won *any* race, game or assignment that I'd ever been involved in. But right now, at least for the next hour or so, I'd be moving slowly whether I wanted to or not.

FOURTEEN

Darkness came quickly and early. It was only six thirty and it was already completely black, the only light coming from the small campfire and the millions of pinprick stars that filled the sky. The three Finns had already turned in for the night. I could hear them talking in their tent. Finnish was certainly a strange language, and I didn't understand a word of it. I didn't understand our porters either. They spoke among themselves in Chachagga, and they seemed to be having a good time, talking and laughing. They seemed very happy and were very friendly—except to me and Sarah. None of them had said a word to me or given me a glance. My things had been carried up, my tent set up, my meal cooked and things were cleaned up, all without a word being exchanged. That left Mr. Odogo, Doris, Sarah and me sitting around the little fire. All the other porters sat well off to the side.

"And you say that this is one of the hardest days," Doris was saying to Mr. Odogo.

"Many think it is the second hardest."

"And which is *the* hardest?" I asked.

"The day we summit. We will rise at midnight and walk six or seven hours to Uhuru Peak so that we can see the sun rise over the summit."

"That sounds lovely," Doris said. "I can't wait."

You might have to wait for another lifetime, I thought.

"And then we must start down," Mr. Odogo continued. "We will walk another seven or eight hours. Some people think down is easy, but for many it is even harder."

Everybody sat quietly around the fire, staring into the flames. There wasn't much more conversation. I thought it was a combination of the thin air and the dead tiredness. I wasn't going to admit it to anyone else, but today's hike had been more than a simple walk in the park. I was tired. As well, my stomach was upset. It grumbled noisily, as if it knew I was thinking about it. Either nobody heard it, or they were being polite and pretending that they didn't.

Slowly I got up. I had to go to the toilet. Again. I felt a little embarrassed. It wasn't like there was really anything to be embarrassed about. We all had to go. I just seemed to be doing it more than anybody else and more than I wanted to.

I knew that the gurgling in my stomach would quickly become a rumbling in my intestines, which would soon become an explosion down below. There was an equation I had to figure out each time. I had to go far enough and fast enough to get privacy, but not so far that I could potentially fall off the side of the mountain.

At least at this elevation, the rainforest behind and below us, there really wasn't much chance of running into a leopard, an elephant or even a semi-poisonous snake. At least that was the conversation that I was having with myself to induce a little bit of confidence. My stomach called out a warning shot, and I hustled a dozen more steps before I ducked down behind a big rock, sure that I was now hidden from those sitting at the campsite. Of course, if that rock was big enough to hide me, wasn't it also big enough to hide a leopard?

I unbuckled my belt, pulled down my pants and squatted down. I hate squatting, but what choice did I have? It wasn't like there was indoor plumbing on the mountain. Going to the toilet hadn't really been something I'd thought about at all before I got here. But now that I was on the mountain, it had become a serious concern. Funny, I wasn't as worried about not reaching the summit or falling off the mountain as I was about having a different type of accident...in my pants.

The cool air chilled my bare butt and I felt myself clench up. Being cold wasn't the best condition for going quickly and I did want to go fast. Being exposed to the elements this way—pants down and squatting—made me felt incredibly vulnerable. I concentrated and things got rolling...well, running. As quickly as possible I finished up, including the paper work. Now I just had to—

"I need to talk to you."

I jumped up, spinning and pulling up my pants all at once. Mr. Odogo was standing in front of me.

"I need to talk to you," he repeated. He didn't look any happier than he sounded.

"Yes, sir, what would you like to talk about?" I asked as I scrambled to do up my belt. This was embarrassing.

"Do you know why I am bringing you up my mountain?"

"Because of my grandfather," I said, thinking about his ashes.

"Because of him and what he did for my father," he said.

"Yes, sir."

"My father informed me that your grandfather was a great man," he said. "Do you think that *you* are a great man?"

I didn't know what to answer. I was shocked and surprised by the question.

Mr. Odogo continued. "Because you are barely a man and greatness has not come to you, nor may it ever."

"Um...yes, sir. I mean, no, sir."

"Do you think you have the right to come to this mountain and give orders?" he asked.

"I haven't given any orders or—"

"You demanded that my daughter be one of your porters, did you not?"

"I don't think I really demanded," I said.

He looked at me questioningly. "My daughter said to me that you *insisted*—demanded—that she come along."

Okay, this was all starting to make sense. This had to do with Sarah—again. It had been nothing but trouble, having her along.

"I didn't really demand…it was more of a polite request."

"Are you calling my daughter a liar?"

"No, sir. I'm just sort of saying that she's… she's very…very…*determined*."

"She gets that from her mother."

"That sounds a lot like *my* mother," I said.

He smiled. Slightly. But even slightly was better than the scowl that had been there.

"So why then did you *politely request* that my daughter be one of your porters?" he asked.

Now I was caught. I couldn't tell him the truth. That would be breaking my word.

"Um, I guess I just wanted somebody around who was my age."

"How old are you?"

"Eighteen, well, at least on my next birthday."

"My daughter is only fourteen. That is *not* the same age."

She had told me she was fifteen, hadn't she? "It's closer than anybody else on this trip."

"Four years. In my country many men marry girls who are four years younger," he said.

"I guess that's true in my country too."

"So is that your intent? Did you invite my daughter along because you wish her to become your wife?"

"No, of course not!" I exclaimed.

"Do you think you are too good for my daughter?"

I was almost too stunned to answer, but I had to. "No, sir, of course not. It's not that I'm too good, sir. It's just that...just that...she really wanted to be a porter and I was trying to make her happy. That's all there is to it, sir, honestly."

His expression didn't change. He stared right into my eyes like he was trying to see inside of me to tell if what I'd said was true. He stepped forward until he was standing so close that our chests were almost touching. I had to fight the urge to step back even though I was so much bigger, so much taller than him that he had to look up at me.

"I think I believe you," he said.

I felt a rush of relief.

"But you need to know," he continued, "that while you are bigger and taller and younger, and probably even stronger, than me, I am her father. If you were to do something that harmed or dishonored my daughter—"

"I would never do that, sir!" I said, cutting him off.

He reached up and placed a hand on my shoulder. "That is good to know." He smiled. "Because this is a high mountain and there are many dangers. I certainly wouldn't want anything bad to happen to you on this climb."

My stomach answered—a big, thundering gurgle that we both heard.

"Maybe you need some more privacy. I will go back to the fire." He turned and walked away.

I took a deep breath. The cool air traced a path down to my lungs. I took another breath. I suddenly felt so very tired. I needed to climb into my tent, get into my sleeping bag and fall asleep—pass out.

My bowels rumbled. One more thing to do first. I undid the buckle one more time.

"Perhaps you should wait a minute before you do that."

I turned around, shocked and surprised again. It was Sarah. Was the whole family going to sneak up on me tonight?

"I followed my father. I overheard."

"You heard him threaten to throw me off the mountain?" I asked. "He wouldn't really do that, would he?"

"Of course not," she offered reassuringly. "He is a guide. He is sworn to protect those he takes up the mountain."

"Yeah, I figured he was just—"

"He would wait until he brought you safely down off the mountain before he was to harm you."

I startled slightly before realizing that she was just fooling…or was she?

"I am grateful you did not tell my father the truth about why you had to bring me. He would not be happy that either of us went out to retrieve your belongings from the street kids."

"I gave you my word." Besides, I didn't want him to be any angrier at me than he already appeared to be.

"Thank you."

She got up on her tiptoes and before I could step away she kissed me on the cheek! What was she doing! If her father saw us, there was no way I was ever going to make it out alive!

"You *are* much too old for me." She walked away, leaving me stunned and scared, and with my bowels about to let loose again. I decided I had better get used to unexpected crap. Of all kinds.

FIFTEEN

Doris and I sat in the little eating tent, finishing up our breakfast. The Finns had already finished and left, which didn't really matter. It wasn't like we could communicate with them.

"You're not eating your porridge," Doris said.

"Calling it porridge is stretching it."

"I must admit I've never eaten anything quite like this before," Doris said.

"I've never *seen* any food this color," I replied. "It's sort of cement gray."

"I think that makes sense. It does taste like what

I imagine cement would taste like. Thank goodness for the sugar."

Doris dropped in another heaping spoonful of brown sugar. I didn't bother. I wasn't going to eat it anyway.

"Even that wouldn't change the texture," I said. "It looks sort of like…like…"

"Diarrhea?"

I nodded. I hadn't wanted to say it.

"At least the fried egg and potatoes are good," I said.

"It would be hard to do those wrong," she agreed. "Although I'm not really sure what this is." She held up the little sausage-like thing they had given us.

"I wonder what type of meat it is?" I said.

"I believe it is wise that we don't ask," she replied. She held up her cup. "Cheers."

We clinked our little plastic cups together and drained the last of our tea.

"Any luck communicating with your family?" she asked.

I pulled out my phone. "Still no signal. I thought once we left the forest we might get something, but nothing."

"Maybe as we climb higher you'll have better luck. We'll certainly be closer to the satellites. That's another reason we should get started. I think we better get ready to leave," Doris suggested.

"Probably not wise to keep Mr. Odogo waiting."

We stepped out to find the porters buzzing around, breaking down the camp. Mr. Odogo was yelling out orders. He didn't seem to need to say the same thing twice. It appeared that I wasn't the only one who was afraid of him. I could have asked one of the porters what he was saying, but there was no way I would have gotten an answer. They were still treating me as if I were invisible. They weren't unfriendly or disrespectful. They just looked right through me. The first of them, loaded down with gear, started up the trail. Right behind him went the three Finns. I guess I wasn't going to be with them on day two either. Actually, Doris was good company. At least she spoke English. I just wished she walked a little faster.

My tent was already packed up. My backpack was sitting where the tent used to be. I slipped it on and had the strangest thought: if I left right now and moved quickly, I could catch the Finns and—

"Do you know what today's journey will be like?" Doris was beside me, her pack on her back, walking sticks in hand.

"From what I read in the guidebook, I think we leave the forest behind completely and spend most of the day walking through heather."

"Wonderful. Our second climatic zone. I'm sure there will still be some flowers."

"We're only walking five or six kilometers, but we gain over eight hundred meters, so it's got to be pretty steep."

"Oh, dear, I hope not too steep."

Mr. Odogo walked over. "We will soon start. This section is very challenging."

"DJ was just explaining that it's quite steep," Doris said.

He looked at me questioningly.

"It's in the guidebook," I explained.

"Perhaps you think because you have a guide-*book* that you do not need a guide."

"No, sir. I just like to know what's coming."

"What is coming is that we need to move *polepole*, and all stay together," he said.

"I don't think that's going to happen."

"What?" he demanded.

"I don't think we're all going to be staying together." I pointed up the slope at the Finns.

He saw them just before they disappeared over a rise. He turned back toward us. He didn't look happy.

"*Mambiri*!" he yelled out, and Sarah came running over. He spoke to her and she nodded repeatedly.

He turned back toward us. "My daughter will guide you. I must go." He rushed after them, moving even faster than the Finns appeared to be moving. I would have loved to move fast. Instead it was going to be another day of *polepole* with Doris as my companion and Sarah as my guide.

The whole world around us changed as we walked. The last vestiges of the cloud forest had completely disappeared and the heath had taken over. Strangely shaped plants, some tall and distorted, others just bushes and brush, dotted the landscape. I couldn't help but think that if Dr. Seuss designed plants, this is what he'd create. Among the plants were rocks carved by wind and rain and time. They were as bizarrely shaped as the plants. More Dr. Seuss.

As well, without trees to block the view, the mountain was a constant presence, looming in front of us. Below, when I was blocked by foliage, I couldn't look far ahead. Here it was impossible to not let my eyes drift forward. The slope we were on was steep but steady. It went on and on until somewhere on the horizon it met the rising grade of the mountain where the white fingers of the glaciers extended down from the top.

I'd read that the first European explorers didn't believe that Kilimanjaro existed because they couldn't possibly imagine snow at the equator. But there it was, so high that at the top it looked and felt polar, even though it was on the equator. I wondered just how cold it was going to be up there. Down here, even two days into the trip I was still wearing a T-shirt and sweating up a storm. The snow didn't seem that real, even though I could see it.

"It is time for a rest," Sarah said.

I was tired but reluctant to stop. I'd been catching glimpses of other climbers up ahead as they appeared and disappeared around rises in the trail. It was another party, and I was positive we were gaining on them.

"Couldn't we go a little bit longer?" I asked.

"I'm okay to continue a little bit longer," Doris said.

"So we can stop in—"

"We stop now," Sarah said, and she halted in her tracks. She turned to face me. "I am the guide."

"I thought you were the porter."

She shook her head. "No wonder my father is annoyed by you."

She unburdened herself of her load. Her two bags were both bigger and bulkier than the little I was carrying on my back. I didn't know how much weight she was carrying, but it was clearly more than I was. She hadn't been complaining, but from the few missteps and stumbles I'd seen, it had to be heavy.

We all pulled out our water bottles and drank. It felt so good. My body was craving the water despite the fact that I'd already guzzled more than a liter. The water didn't just quench my thirst, it also seemed to settle my stomach, which had been grumbling and gurgling all morning. That breakfast just hadn't been enough. If they served that same porridge tomorrow, I'd have to follow Doris's lead and spoon on enough sugar to make it edible. Maybe the secret would be to close my eyes while I ate.

"Sarah," Doris said, "I notice that your father doesn't usually call you Sarah...he calls you Mambi... Mambir..."

"Mambiri," she said. "It is my Chagga name."

"I know that Chagga names most often have meaning. Does your name have a special meaning?" Doris asked.

"It means ripe melon."

"You're a ripe melon?" I chuckled.

"At least I have a name!" she snapped. "Not like you, who only has initials!"

"Initials stand for names. My name is David."

"That is the D, but what is the J?"

"It's Junior. I'm named after my grandfather and I got called David Junior and then it was shortened to DJ."

She shrugged. "At least that makes sense. It is good to be named after your ancestors. My name is that of my mother and grandmother. We Chagga believe that we were created in a melon patch, so many of us are named because of that. Of course it is just a story. We here in Tanzania know the difference between males and females and where babies come from." She gave me a sly little smile.

"Whatever you say, my little ripe Mambiri," I joked.

"It is a very pretty name," Doris said. "Would you mind if I called you Mambiri instead of Sarah?"

"They are both my names. I know it pleases my father when I am called by my Chagga name." She turned to me. "Perhaps you should call me that too... unless he thinks you are being forward because you have designs on me."

"Great, just what I need."

"I just think it's so unfair that DJ is being treated so badly," Doris said. "I think it's actually gallant for him to do as he did."

"Gallant? I do not know that word."

"It means brave, gentlemanly, treating a young woman with respect. He was gallant to invite you along," she explained.

I was none of the above—at least not right now. It hadn't been bravery but stupidity and a total lack of understanding. If I'd known all the trouble it was going to cause, I would have insisted on her *not* coming along. Doris didn't know about Sarah basically blackmailing me and keeping me in the dark, but Sarah certainly did.

I turned at the sound of somebody coming up the trail behind us. It was five climbers, bookended by two guides. Three of the climbers appeared to be in their twenties or early thirties. The other two were a couple in their fifties. Old, but not as old as Doris. I hated the idea of being passed, but at least they could see that Doris was with us—a built-in excuse for stopping that didn't involve me.

The guide called out a big *Jambo* and offered a smile. Then he saw Sarah and the smile faded. He said something to her in Chachagga and they had a rapid-fire exchange. The guide at the back didn't say anything but looked equally annoyed.

"I didn't understand the guide," Doris said, when the other group had moved on, "but he didn't seem particularly friendly."

"What did he say?" I asked Sarah.

"He had heard that there was a female porter on the mountain but he did not believe it until he saw me. He said he wasn't surprised to see me sitting because women sit so much when they wash clothes and cook. He told me it was not too late to go home."

"What a jerk," I said.

"And what did you say to him?" Doris asked.

"I told him he probably wasn't smart enough to do either of those things himself, or handsome enough to attract a woman who would do them for him."

"That must have been when he stopped smiling," I said.

"He then told me I should respect my elders. I told him that respect is earned and not given because of numbers on a calendar."

"You really have a way of making friends," I said.

"Who would want to be friends with such a man?" she said.

"Do you know what would be even better?" I said. "Let's catch up and pass them."

Sarah smiled. Doris got to her feet and said, "I think that would be simply brilliant!"

Time and distance blurred together. Yesterday's hike was a walk in the park compared to today's march. What made it even worse was that over an hour and a half ago the end had been in sight. We had seen our camp up on a plateau. But what we didn't know—what even Sarah didn't know—was that we had to descend over 300 meters down a gorge and then climb back up to the plateau. Going down wasn't easy, and it was made worse knowing that each step downward would translate into a step up on the other side. I *hated* that.

The last part before we hit the bottom was the hardest. Our path was a small stream running down from one of the glaciers, so cold that there were little patches of ice. What a combination to have underfoot: water, ice and slippery wet mud. A few times I'd come close to slip-sliding down onto my butt.

The thing that kept us all moving was wanting to keep in front of that rude guide and his party. I wish I could have taken a picture of his face as we passed them while they sat having lunch. We stopped just after that for a few minutes to get our own lunches out, but we kept moving, *polepole*, and ate as we walked. That suited me, and, really, it wasn't like I had much of an appetite.

We finally reached the bottom of the gorge, which wasn't at all flat, and Sarah didn't hesitate. She just started up the other side.

I turned to Doris. "Are you all right to climb or do you need a little break?"

"Up might feel good," she said. "At least for a little while."

I was happy to keep moving, but I might have been even happier to rest. I was starting to realize that, more and more often, Doris was asking to stop just before I would have asked. I was feeling tired, my legs heavy, and my whole digestive system was keeping up a steady symphony of sounds.

Suddenly Sarah stumbled, toppled forward and fell down! I rushed forward as she struggled to regain her footing. She got to her knees before I could reach her.

"Are you okay?"

"Sorry, sorry," she said. She looked embarrassed.

"Here," I said, offering her a hand. I was surprised when she didn't brush it away. I pulled her to her feet.

"I am fine," Sarah said. "We need to go."

"No," Doris said. "I need to rest. I need a break."

"I could use a rest too." I pulled off my pack and set it down on the ground. "Let me help you with your load," I said to Sarah.

I went to help her remove the first pack. I half expected her to argue, but she didn't.

"Wow, this is incredibly heavy!" I exclaimed as I set it down and then helped her with the second, which was equally heavy.

"I can't believe all the porters carry this much weight," I said.

"They do not," she said.

"Some are carrying more?"

She shook her head. "I am carrying the most."

I was shocked and speechless.

"Does your father know they are making you carry more?" Doris asked.

"He knows."

It was wrong that the other porters were treating her so badly, but to get that treatment from her own father? That was just mean. Giving me a hard time was one thing, but that was no way to treat his daughter. It wasn't very gallant.

SIXTEEN

I was tired. So tired. And sore and achy and my stomach was upset and I'd gone to the toilet four times and I had had to force myself to eat supper. Other than that I was fine. What I needed to do was go to bed. It was only seven thirty, but it was dark. I was about to climb into my little tent and curl up in the sleeping bag when Mr. Odogo walked into the camp. I had something I wanted to do before I slept. He wouldn't like what I had to say, but what did it matter? Unless he was going to throw me off the mountain, he couldn't really treat me any worse.

"Excuse me, Mr. Odogo," I called out.

He turned, nodded and came in my direction.

"How was your day's trek?" he asked.

That sounded friendly. Voice, expression and question. What was going on?

"It was good. Hard but good."

"Mambiri said you are doing well."

"*She's* doing well," I said. "You must be proud of her," I added.

"I have always been most proud of her. She is a good daughter."

I thought for a second and then decided to jump in. "Then why are you making her carry more than the other porters?"

"That is the way things must be done," he said.

"Because she's the youngest she has to carry the most? That isn't fair."

"She is carrying the most because she is the newest. The newest porter always must prove himself and carry the heaviest load. Even if that porter is my child. Even if that porter is my *daughter*. That *is* fair." He paused. "Are you questioning my decisions or orders?"

"No. I mean, I guess I was. I understand, now that you explained it. It's just that it's so hard for her."

"It is not easy for me to witness," he said. "But it is the way it must be. She is lucky to have a friend along who cares. Thank you."

"Um, you're welcome."

He put a hand on my shoulder. "But you are not to question any more of my decisions. Understand?"

"Yes, sir."

"Good. Now go to bed. You look tired."

SEVENTEEN

Doris was standing at the edge of the camp, looking off into the distance. She'd been there for a long time. I wanted to give her some privacy, but I was a little worried. Quietly I walked over until I was right behind her. I cleared my throat to let her know I was there, and she turned around.

"Good morning," she said.

"A little chillier than I thought it would be."

"We are gaining altitude," she said. "I was just thinking how much my husband, Samuel, would have loved being here."

"My grandpa too. It was his dream to climb Kilimanjaro."

"Samuel's too. I guess because it wasn't mine, he never got to realize his. Did you ever think about climbing this mountain?" she asked.

I shook my head. "Never thought about it. Probably never would have."

"It's sad that the two who wanted most to climb it never did, and the two who didn't are climbing it," she said. "Sometimes life works out that way."

I didn't know what to say. Not that I thought she was wrong.

"It is beautiful," she said.

I looked out over the edge of the plateau to where she was staring. It was amazing, although I didn't know if I'd use the word *beautiful* to describe it. It was stark, desolate, filled with rocks broken up by only an occasional cluster of stunted trees. And of course in the distance was the summit.

I saw it more as an obstacle, something I had to overcome to get to where I was going, than a thing of beauty. I thought about what my grandfather had written—about enjoying the steps along the way.

Did that really apply to everything? Should you enjoy going to the dentist, having a headache—which I had now—going to a funeral, or climbing a mountain? Sure, I had goals and dreams, but climbing this mountain wasn't one of them. Sure, I was going to do it, but did that mean I had to enjoy it? It seemed more like something that I had to endure. Like training camp or practice. Nobody enjoyed those. You just did it so you could get to the game.

"Our Finnish friends don't seem as chipper this morning," Doris said.

"They were a little less enthusiastic," I agreed. "I guess we're all a little tired."

"That's almost reassuring. I was beginning to think it was only me."

"I've felt better. It all starts to wear you down after a while," I admitted.

"I guess all we can do is eat, drink, rest and try to stay strong. After all, we have a couple of people counting on us. We can't let them down now, can we?"

"I guess not."

"Perhaps we better get ready to go."

"The sooner we start, the sooner we finish," I said.

Polepole. Polepole. Polepole. It was starting to be like a rhythmic chant in my head as each porter who passed us imparted those words of wisdom. It felt more like a taunt. They raced by, carrying and balancing loads on their heads and backs, and told us that we were slow and they were fast. I would have argued if it wasn't so obviously true. It still didn't make me like it any more.

A couple of times I'd tried to pick up my pace, staying with them and leaving Doris behind. And every time I had to abandon the attempt because my legs and lungs just couldn't keep up. I hated it, but I had no choice. Mr. Odogo had pretty well given up on the Finns—they couldn't really understand much English so he couldn't control them—but he still was intent on keeping me from going too fast. At least instead of looking like a loser, it looked like I was following orders—*polepole*—or being kind to Doris. I had to admit that she was pretty easy to be kind to. She was a nice old lady. So it was me, one nice old lady and our guide in a little line, going up the mountain.

Earlier in the day one of the other trails up the mountain had merged with ours. That meant that the number of climbing parties had doubled. It wasn't really crowded, but it was definitely more populated. Occasionally we passed other parties or were passed by them during rest breaks, but mostly we saw porters. There were a lot of them, and each carried a heavy load: bags, barrels, chairs and tables, large cartons of eggs, cookstoves, and in one case a toilet—a *sit-down* toilet. It seemed so unnecessary and so wonderful all at once. I wondered if I could rent it.

I liked when we passed porters from other parties. They didn't know that they shouldn't be friendly with me. They yelled out greetings and encouragement, and despite the sweat and strain they were smiling and happy. They were always talking among themselves, laughing and sometimes singing.

"It is time to rest," Mr. Odogo finally said.

I was grateful. I had wanted to stop for the past twenty minutes but didn't want to be the one to ask. We pulled off our packs and sat down on some rocks. There was never a shortage of rocks to rest on.

"We will have afternoon tea," he said as he pulled a thermos out of his pack.

"That seems so *civilized*," Doris said.

"My grandpa used to say that."

"One of the best things left to us by the British was tea," Mr. Odogo said. "Shame that there are not crumpets and scones and marmalade to go along."

"When we get back to the hotel, perhaps we can share afternoon tea," Doris suggested.

"That would be most wonderful," he agreed.

"And we can raise a toast to our successful summit," she added. "Mine, DJ's and, of course, Mambiri's."

"We always celebrate all who reach the summit."

"When did you celebrate your first summit?" Doris asked.

"Many, many years ago," he said and laughed. "I was only twelve."

"So even younger than your daughter."

"Even younger. I climbed with my grandfather."

"That must have made it even more special," Doris said.

Mr. Odogo nodded his head and smiled at the memory. It was becoming more obvious what Doris was doing—trying to make him feel better about Sarah being along. I couldn't get away with it.

"We need to finish our tea and continue, or none of us will summit," Mr. Odogo said.

I got up to my feet. I wasn't really ready, but I couldn't let anybody know—especially Mr. Odogo.

EIGHTEEN

The pressure in my bladder woke me up again. I didn't want to get up. My sleeping bag was warm and outside wasn't. I wanted to lie there and wait for my body to somehow *reabsorb* my urine, but I wasn't tired enough to be able to convince myself that was possible. Sooner or later I was going to have to get up, and the sooner I did, the sooner I could get back to sleep.

I crawled out of the sleeping bag and slipped on my sandals. I was already wearing so many clothes I didn't bother putting on my jacket. It was cold, and it was going to get colder as we kept climbing.

When I clicked on my headlamp, the tent was bathed in light. The tent zipper stuck and then opened loudly, the only sound in a silent night.

I crawled out of the tent and was greeted by the cold air and the damp mist that still clung to the ground, obscuring my view. It was the same fog that had been with us since we had arrived at the campsite—although it wasn't really fog. It was a cloud. We were sleeping at cloud level.

The light from my headlamp bounced back after a meter or two, leaving me unable to see much ahead of me. Aside from my tent, the rocky ground at my feet, and Doris's tent next to me, I could see nothing else. I could have been anywhere. Thank goodness I didn't need much more than a place to empty my bladder.

I sidestepped around the rocks and between the tents. In this thick mist, two dozen steps away would leave me lost. I could fall off the mountain or—more realistically—not be able to find my way back to my tent. I wasn't going to chance either. Still in sight of my tent, I began to relieve myself.

It was a thick, long stream that kept coming and coming and coming. That was good. Water in and water out meant that I was hydrated. Never before had I been so aware of my urine. Never before had I had so much of it to be aware of. Increased altitude just pushed it out of you.

I tucked myself back in and did a quick physical inventory, starting at the bottom. My feet were fine except for one little blister on the little toe of the left foot and a bruise on the big toe of my right foot where I'd kicked a rock. Sore but okay. I still hadn't taken my sock off to have a look.

Next were my ankles. Fine: no twists, no sprains, no strains. Knees were good, a little sore, but they were always a little sore. Football did that to a guy.

I took a deep breath. My lungs filled with the cool air. No problems breathing; it felt very natural. It was different when I was climbing, but as long as it returned to normal when at rest, I was okay.

Next I placed a hand on my heart. Slow, steady, regular beat. No problems there either. My head was a little achy. I had a slight throbbing at the base of my head but figured that had more to do with my neck being kinked when I slept than it did with mountain sickness.

Finally, I did feel a bit tired, but what could I expect? I'd climbed close to 2,400 meters and walked almost 25 kilometers. I deserved to be tired. And the only cure for that was to get back to sleep.

I couldn't believe how focused I was on how my various body parts were functioning. Never had eating, sleeping, eliminating wastes and inventorying my body parts taken up so much of my attention. Normally anybody this concerned should consult a doctor—a psychiatrist, probably—but of course this situation was far from normal.

As I stood there, I realized that the cloud was dispersing. I could see farther and more clearly. Above me the moon poked free of the clouds. It was nearly full—bright and white and glowing. Around it little pinpricks of stars became visible, filling the night sky and adding to the natural light. I turned off my headlamp, and I could see better without it.

I was standing on a fairly flat plateau that held nine little tents. Over to the edge, on one of the drop-offs, stood the outhouse. Even in the dark it looked neither safe nor solid. In the other direction I could pick out other lights, not from the sky but from the ground. They were the lights of civilization. Was that the town of Moshi down there...way down there?

Behind me, pressing in, was a solid wall of rock. I tipped back my head, following it up, looking for a top I couldn't see, lost in the darkness and distance. It was high; I just couldn't tell how high. I didn't know which way we'd be traveling tomorrow, but I did know which direction we *wouldn't* be going. But regardless of the direction, I had to get back to my tent and sleep as long as I could, until my bladder forced me out of my sleeping bag again.

NINETEEN

I slurped down a little porridge and then stopped. I just couldn't stomach it. Seeing it every morning didn't make it any less disgusting. It still looked more like something that should have been coming out the other end of me rather than going into my mouth.

I took another bite of my breakfast "sausage" and took a sip of tea to clear my mouth of both the last of the mystery meat and the vestiges of the porridge.

This was our third breakfast—our third i*dentical* breakfast. Sarah had said it was going to be the same each morning until we were back at the hotel. One more reason to get through as quickly as possible.

If I lost my appetite, it would have nothing to do with altitude sickness.

I had one more task to accomplish: onward to the toilet. I left the breakfast tent and immediately saw the three Finns. They saw me, waved and smiled. They were relentlessly friendly and smiling even though we couldn't actually communicate.

I approached the toilet with trepidation. It was a small wooden building constructed over the *edge* of the cliff. It looked as if a strong breeze would blow it away. That was more than just paranoid thinking. Mr. Odogo had told me that two years ago one of these little shacks did tumble over, killing the man who was inside. Death in a falling toilet would have been so embarrassing. What would they say at the funeral that wouldn't sound awkward, awful or just plain funny?

I pushed open the door. Of course there was nothing except a hole in the bottom to squat over. I didn't expect anything more but kept wondering what people around here had against sitting down? Using just one foot, I stepped partway in and pressed my weight against the floor. It seemed solid. Hesitantly I put the other foot inside and tried to close the door. It was stuck. I pushed harder and it gave way. The entire shack shook and the door closed, trapping me inside. I had to fight the urge to jump back out, but I had business to do and the way my stomach and intestines were gurgling, it wasn't going to take long.

I pulled down my pants and long johns, and then, bracing myself with a hand on both sides, squatted down. There was a cold breeze coming up through the hole that didn't make it any more pleasant. I tried to focus on the matters at hand and not the hole or the breeze or the fact that I was standing on a little piece of wood perched over a cliff. Thank goodness I didn't have to wait too long. It felt like the porridge was pouring out the other end. I didn't look to see if it was still gray. I didn't care. It was coming out. I just hoped most of it was hitting the hole instead of bouncing back at me.

Moving one hand to grab a baby wipe from the package in my pocket, I almost toppled over. Squatting was not part of my routine or my muscle memory. I finished up the paper work and somebody pounded on the door! I jumped straight up, grabbing my pants and trying to secure the door.

"Are you going to spend the day in there?" Sarah said.

"Are you going to make a habit of bothering me while I'm using the toilet?" I asked. "Can't you bear being away from me even for a few seconds?"

There was a loud huffing sound and she was gone. I finished pulling up both layers of clothing. I realized that my legs were shaking, and I was sweating. Instant flop sweat. Instant fear reaction. She had scared me. I wiped my forehead with the sleeve of my sweater. I had to compose myself. I took a deep breath and realized that maybe the best way to get calm was to get out of the outhouse and back on solid rock.

The door opened, rubbing against the floor, slightly rocking the whole structure again. I jumped out and was relieved in a whole different way.

The porters were moving around the camp, working as hard as ants, disassembling the camp. The tents were coming down quickly, and my backpack was sitting on the ground, leaning against a rock where my tent had been. I noticed that the Finns already had their packs on. I went over and slipped on mine. Nobody—meaning Sarah or her father—could accuse me this morning of not being ready to go.

I was ready, willing and at least semi-able. Not that I'd let them know that.

I walked over to Mr. Odogo, who was yelling out orders to the porters.

"I'm ready," I said. "Maybe I could go with them." I pointed at the Finns.

"Maybe you should just do what you are told. Do you want to get to the top?"

"Of course I do. They seem to be doing okay."

"They have not yet come to the wall," he said.

I'd heard about marathon runners "hitting the wall" when they had run close to twenty miles. I didn't see these three hitting any wall, but I still wondered.

"When do you think they'll hit the wall?" I asked.

"In about ten minutes," he answered.

"How can you be so certain about the timing?"

He gave me a confused look. "The wall," he said, gesturing to the cliff. "We are going to climb the wall this morning."

"We're climbing that?"

"Unless you know of another option."

I looked at the wall. Here in the light of day I could look up, all the way up to the top.

"But—but that has to be *two hundred* meters tall."

"Two hundred and forty meters."

I tried to hide my feelings of fear and disbelief. He had to be joking, making fun of me.

"I don't see a trail."

"It is there. Some places it is very, very narrow, but there is a way up the Breakfast Wall."

"It's called the Breakfast Wall?"

"Some call it Barranco Wall because this is Barranco camp. I like to call it the Breakfast Wall for two reasons. One, we always climb it right after breakfast." He stopped talking.

"And the second reason?"

"Many people lose their breakfast while climbing," he said. "We will soon find out if you are one of them."

TWENTY

I stayed as close to the cliff face as possible, keeping the width of the narrow path between me and the drop at the other side. The Finns, who had to stay with us through the climb, occasionally looked over the edge, laughing and pointing and taking pictures. I wasn't looking, I wasn't laughing and I wasn't taking pictures. I needed both my hands free to cling to the handholds on the rock face.

The path snaked back and forth across the face of the cliff. At times it was almost level and wide, and then it would shoot upward and narrow until it was impossible to be away from the drop.

With each step up, each meter of elevation gained, the drop got bigger. At this point, almost an hour into the climb, it really didn't matter. Fall over the edge and you were dead, whether it was 50 meters or 150 meters...actually it was probably more than 150 meters because we were more than two-thirds of the way up.

At least that's what Mr. Odogo had told us. I just didn't know if I could believe him. He was always underestimating the time or distance left. I'd learned that "twenty minutes" meant closer to an hour. I knew he wasn't lying, but he was either telling us what we needed to hear to encourage us or was actually telling us the time it would have taken us if we didn't have to keep stopping. And in this section we kept stopping.

Doris was having some serious problems. Mr. Odogo was carrying her backpack, and repeatedly he had taken her hand, helped her up a section, or used his body as a shield, standing between her and the edge. I almost envied her, although if I tripped, I didn't think he'd be big enough to stop me from going over. I'd just take him with me and have company on the way down to our shared deaths.

Doris called for another stop. I was grateful. Not just that we were stopping but for the location she'd chosen. It was a fairly flat, wide section of trail, and there were even spots to rest with our backs against the cliff face. Doris took a seat, and I slumped down beside her.

"How are you doing?" I asked.

"Slow but steady, although I can't seem to find any flowers to smell."

"Maybe it's time to take pictures of rocks," I suggested.

"If I did that, there would be no shortage of photo opportunities."

I pulled out my water bottle and took a big slug of water. My breathing had quickly settled back to normal, but I could feel my heart pounding heavily. My lungs were responding to the rest, but my heart wasn't. It was still reacting to the fact that we were on the side of a cliff and I was feeling fear. Pure fear. Why had my grandpa sent the kid who was afraid of heights up the side of a mountain?

"This is a little bit like having a baby," Doris said.

"It is?"

"Yes. It's a great deal of hard work; you take it one contraction at a time; and once you start, you really can't stop until it's over."

I laughed nervously. "I guess I'm going to have to take your word for it."

"You make sure you're there with your wife when she has your babies. No loafing about in the waiting room."

"I won't do that."

"I didn't expect that you would. You don't seem the sort to shirk from work or responsibilities," she said.

"I try to do the right thing."

"Even if it means waiting for an old woman to climb the mountain?" she asked.

"It's not a problem for me," I said. "Them I'm not too sure about."

I gestured to the three Finns. They seemed to be doing better than they had been at the start of the day. They were on their feet, packs on, edging forward even while they were waiting. Actually I was grateful that Doris was here. Otherwise it would have been obvious that I was the weak link, and they would have been waiting for me. Now I could at least look gracious, staying with her, rather than being a weight holding everybody else back. I was tired and sluggish, and my feet—my incredibly big feet—were clumsy.

"Here come the porters," Doris said as she leaned forward to look over the edge.

I didn't need to look. I could hear them. They were talking among themselves and their footfalls were loud, moving fast even with heavy weights on their backs. The first poked his head over the edge of the ridge below us. On his head was balanced a load of gear. I knew that even if it was heavy, it wasn't as heavy as what Sarah was carrying.

He pulled himself up to reveal that he had a pack strapped to his front and his back. It looked like the weight he was carrying was greater than his body weight. Of course, putting the two numbers together, he still didn't weigh much more than I did if I didn't have a pack on at all. There was sweat pouring down his brow and dripping from his face. It was almost reassuring to see that this climb wasn't effortless for him.

We pressed closer against the cliff face to allow him to pass along the narrow path with his wide load.

"*Jambo, assante sana*," he called out to Doris, offering her a smile.

"*Karibu*," she replied.

"*Jambo*," I said.

He looked at me and his smile disappeared. The same thing happened as each porter passed—friendly to Doris, openly ignoring me. I had obviously gained the superhero power of invisibility. At least with our porters.

"They really are being particularly nasty toward you," Doris said. "And this is all because you asked for Sarah to come on this journey."

I nodded. "At least they're not discriminating. They're not talking to her either."

"These fellows should all be ashamed of themselves. Don't any of them have daughters or wives? I know they all must have mothers."

"Remember, they believe they came from a melon patch," I offered.

"Even melons have mothers. They should show both you and Sarah more courtesy and kindness."

"Where is Sarah?"

I looked back down the path. All the other porters had passed. Just then, as if on cue, she poked her head over the top of the ledge. She strained—little muscles on pencil-thin arms—to pull herself up. Her load looked much larger than that of anybody who had passed. Larger and heavier.

"*Jambo*," she said. Her breath was strained and her face was beaded with sweat.

"You okay?" I asked.

"She is fine!"

I turned around. It was Mr. Odogo.

"She is both a Chagga and a porter, so she is fine," he said.

I wish I'd known he was so close or I wouldn't have said anything.

"I am fine," Sarah agreed.

"Although she would be finer if she could be with the other porters. You must hurry your pace."

He was speaking to her but looking directly at me, daring me to say something, to challenge him. I didn't. I didn't really think he'd push me off a mountain, but if he had wanted to, there was no better place.

"We all need to go," Mr. Odogo ordered.

I offered Doris my hand to help her to her feet.

"Thank you," she said. "*You* are a gentleman."

We started climbing again.

I pulled myself up over the rise, and I could hardly believe my eyes. We were at the top of the wall! Stretching out in front of me was a long, steady incline. We still had to climb, but we'd finished the Breakfast Wall. It had taken us just over two and a half hours to climb the 240 meters of cliff. I was so happy, so thrilled, to be done that I almost started to giggle.

"We did it," I said with satisfaction.

"Yes, you have scaled the wall," Mr. Odogo said. "You have finished the very *first* part of our day's safari."

I'd been so focused on the wall that I'd lost track of the fact that it was only the beginning leg on today's trip. "How much farther is it?"

"Not much. Four hours if we move fast, not counting a break for lunch."

"But how far is it? How much farther do we have to go?"

"Are you tired?" he asked.

I almost lied but didn't, because it never came naturally. I nodded.

"Then you will be much more tired at the end of this day. It is a *very* hard day."

"Harder than the summit day?" I asked.

He laughed. "No day is harder than the summit."

"Really?"

"Are you questioning my word again?"

"No...no, sir. It's just that the Breakfast Wall was *really* hard."

"It is hard but it is not high."

"There's a taller wall to climb than that one?" I gasped.

"Not *taller*, but *higher*."

Now I was just as confused as I was tired. "I don't understand."

"The Breakfast Wall, the Barranco Wall, is the tallest single climb, at over two hundred and forty meters tall, but it is not the highest."

"Okay, you're saying it's the tallest but not the highest. I don't understand how that can be possible."

He gave me the kind of look usually reserved for when you are trying to explain something very simple to a small child.

"It is tall, but it is also low. It starts at just below four thousand meters in height and then ends at four thousand two hundred and twenty. It is not high. It is low. High is the top of the mountain at five thousand eight hundred and ninety-five meters. So the wall is tall, but it is still not high. Do you understand?"

"Now I do."

"You will see high and you will *feel* high as we climb. Nobody gets mountain sickness at three thousand meters. It starts now and with each step there is more chance. You will find that out."

Or maybe I had already been finding that out.

"The secret is to go *polepole*."

"I think you're preaching to the wrong people," Doris said. She pointed toward the Finns who had gotten up from their rest and were already well along the trail, leaving us all behind.

Mr. Odogo muttered something under his breath, and his face changed into the expression of annoyance he usually reserved for me. He called out and the porters, who were sitting in two groups—Sarah by herself and the others all together—all got quickly got to their feet.

"I must catch those men and try to counsel them," Mr. Odogo said.

I almost blurted out that they seemed to be doing fine without him but was smart enough to keep my mouth shut. At least this once.

"I have ordered the porters to go forward to set up camp," he said. "Except for one. She will be your guide for this portion of the trip."

She could only mean one person. I was happy about that. There were lots of people in our group but only two other people on my team—Sarah and Doris.

"You must listen to her and remember to take it all slowly. You must remember that with each step you are closer to the top, but that each step is harder than the one before."

"That's not a very reassuring thought," I said, once again instantly regretting the words as they escaped my mouth.

"Do you want reassurance or honesty?" he demanded.

"Honesty, sir."

"Good. Now I must leave."

He turned to leave, yelling out a few words in Chachagga to Sarah as she came toward us. She replied, nodding her head. She looked as tired as I felt. Leading the porters, Mr. Odogo quickly set off on the path chasing the three Finns, who were almost out of sight. I had no doubt that he'd catch them but didn't understand why he was so upset with them. They seemed to be doing just fine without him.

"We must leave too," Sarah said.

Doris was already on her feet, ready to go. She was a real trooper. I pulled on my pack and was ready to go as well.

It was strange, but I almost started to miss the climb of the Breakfast Wall. The slope we were on was much gentler but seemed to be without end. Short and steep now seemed more appealing. I never thought I'd think that.

Sarah led, followed by Doris and then me. As we traveled, it was apparent that Sarah was struggling even more under the load she was carrying.

A few times she stumbled, once again almost toppling over before regaining her footing. She was sweating profusely and her breathing didn't seem that much easier than mine or Doris's. I was feeling increasingly guilty. It just didn't seem right to allow a girl—one who was younger and smaller and weaker than me—to carry so much more than me. I knew what she was going to say and that I'd regret asking, but I had to.

"Sarah, I was thinking that if you needed a little help I could—"

"I do not need any help!" she snapped, cutting me off.

"It's just that you look like you're really—"

"Would you offer to carry some of the load of another porter?" she demanded.

"I would if they looked tired and started to stumble."

"You need not worry about anybody except yourself. You need to just walk. By the end of the day I might have to carry you!"

"No need to take offence," I said. "You are just such a sensitive little *melon*. Are you feeling a bit overripe, Mambiri?"

Sarah turned and scowled at me. I smiled back, and she seemed to be working hard to keep the scowl in place. Finally the scowl broke into a smile.

"Could we take a short break?" Doris asked.

I knew Doris was tired, but I think she was trying to help Sarah not lose face.

"We should rest," Sarah agreed. "And eat. It is almost time for lunch break, so we can eat now."

We each put down our loads and took seats on the rocks that littered the route. Sarah went into one of the packs she was carrying and pulled out something wrapped in aluminum foil and then a large thermos and three cups.

"It is chicken and tea," she said.

She unfolded the foil, revealing three pieces of chicken, and then handed us each one. It was the same chicken we'd had yesterday for lunch. It had been dried in a way that it didn't need refrigeration. At the same time, Doris poured out three cups of tea—the sugar and milk already added.

"I know the other porters are not pleased with you being here, but I find it such a pleasure to have another female along," Doris said.

"It is good to be here...although not a pleasure. Much work. It is very hard."

"I never thought I'd hear you say that," I said.

"It is hard, but I will succeed."

"I wish I had that confidence," Doris said.

"Confidence is good, but I have seen many, many fat people who have made the top."

"Fat people climb this mountain?" I asked.

"Yes, some who are even fatter than you."

"Me? I'm not fat!"

"How much do you weigh?"

"I weigh around one hundred kilograms," I said.

"That is even fatter than I thought! You are fatter than me and my brother and baby sister all put together."

"That's because I'm taller and bigger than the three of you put together. This isn't fat, this is muscle," I protested, holding up my arm.

"I do not think so. If you had muscle, you could carry more on your back."

"I *offered* to take some more of the load."

"It is no good making an offer you cannot fulfill. You are having enough trouble moving yourself, so we cannot talk about extra weight. Now eat your chicken."

I looked at the piece of chicken. It had absolutely no appeal for me. "I don't think so. I'm too fat to eat any more."

"You are fat, but you need to eat," she said. "I am only your guide. Do not make me act like your mother or your wife. I pity the first and question whether you will ever have the second."

Doris chuckled.

"He is like a little baby who needs to be cared for," Sarah said to Doris. Then she turned back to me. "You did not eat much breakfast either. Do you not have an appetite?"

"Not for this."

"If you wish to summit tomorrow you need to eat today. It does not matter if you have an appetite; you *must* eat."

"If I eat, will you leave me alone?"

"Start eating and I will decide."

I picked at the chicken and used my other hand to rub the back of my neck. The stiffness was spreading right up into the base of my head.

"Are you all right?" Doris asked. "You look like you're in pain."

"I've got a bit of a headache. It feels like my head is a bit swollen."

As soon as I said it, I realized that it could mean more than just sleeping funny.

"A swollen head?" Sarah asked. "That could be because of the altitude or because you always have a swollen head."

"Or it could just mean I have a headache. I get those occasionally, even at home."

Doris began to laugh and then stopped. "I'm sorry," she said. "I don't find your headache funny. But you two act like an old married couple."

"Us?" I gasped.

"Yes. It's as if you both enjoy these little spats, but neither of you means what you say."

"I do not wish to fight with him, but somebody has to tell him what to do," Sarah said. "He is practically helpless."

"My Samuel always said a good husband needs to listen to his wife," Doris said.

"Could we just finish eating so we can get to the base camp?" I asked, desperate to change the subject.

"For once he is right," Sarah said. "We need to get to the camp as early as possible so that you both can rest. Sleep will be short before you attack the summit."

I tried to force down the rest of my chicken. I didn't have an appetite, my head was hurting and my stomach was feeling uneasy. I had to convince myself that none of these things meant anything, but I didn't have much success.

By the time we reached camp, the tents were already up and supper was waiting for us. The three Finns had eaten and gone to bed. I wanted to go to bed, but I had to eat. I tried to force down the meal. It was different than the others. There was a big plate of fried potatoes mixed with eggs. This was the meal that was supposed to power me to the top. Instead it just turned my stomach. I had to walk a fine line: eat enough to give me power but not so much that my stomach would throw it all back up.

I was tired. My muscles were sore. And then there was the headache. It had grown and spread until it was the whole back of my head and was starting to migrate along both sides and toward the front.

Add in the poor appetite and feeling nauseous, and I was the poster child for mountain sickness. But still, it was only one more day—really only one more night of climbing. I'd written my final exams last year when I was under the weather. I'd played a football game when I had a high fever. I could play through sickness. Of course this wasn't just playing a game, this was climbing a mountain. The best thing to do was to get to sleep and recharge my batteries. When I woke up, I'd feel better.

I pushed away the food, half eaten, got up and headed toward my tent. If I went straight to sleep, I'd get almost four hours before they woke me. Before we started for the summit. I knew the start was certain. I just wasn't feeling very positive about the ending. Could I really do this?

TWENTY-ONE

I was startled out of my restless sleep by the sounds of people outside my tent. It must be time to leave. Time to get to the summit. At least this time I was woken up by something outside of my own faulty, leaking bodily functions. I'd been up three times already—once to vomit, another time to pee, and a third as my bowels ran. If my body was going to betray me, why couldn't all three systems have exploded at once? It would have been more efficient.

I pulled myself out of my sleeping bag. Even that process of shifting a few feet caused my heart to race and my breath to strain. That was partly the altitude and partly my fear—not fear of the mountain but fear I was going to fail. Fail. Did I really think I could make it up to the top feeling the way I felt?

I switched on the headlamp and the tent became brightly illuminated. I glanced at my watch. It was just after eleven. We weren't going to be leaving until midnight. I could sleep for another hour. I thought about turning off the light and lying back down, but the voices were getting louder and more frantic. Something was happening, and it wasn't like I was actually going to go back to sleep anyway.

I was already fully dressed to protect myself from the cold—three layers top and bottom, including thermal underwear and fleece. All I had to do was pull on my hat, mitts and hiking boots. I struggled with the laces—my fingers felt a little numb—and then unzipped the tent. A rush of wind and cold air flooded in.

The campsite was alive with porters frantically racing around. I guess they were as excited about the summit as I was. No, wait...there was Tomas, one of the Finns, sitting on the ground, Mr. Odogo standing over him. As I watched, he started to vomit violently—projectile puking, really—strangely illuminated by his headlamp.

His body heaved again and he puked a second time. Mountain sickness; he was suffering from mountain sickness too.

I saw Sarah and went over to stand at her side. "Mountain sickness?" I asked quietly.

"Yes, him and both of the others. One very bad too." She gestured to the other two Finns, one lying flat on his back and the other doubled over beside him.

"They're really sick, aren't they?" I asked.

"I think they are very bad, but I have never seen mountain sickness."

"But they were doing so well," I said.

"It means nothing until you reach four thousand meters," she said. "Let's get closer."

I followed her over, but neither of us spoke. Mr. Odogo was too busy and things seemed too serious to interrupt him. He was barking out orders to the porters. They were using poles and canvas to construct what looked like stretchers. Were they going to carry them down the mountain?

As we stood and watched, we were joined by Doris.

"Mountain sickness," I explained.

"Oh, dear," she said. "They were looking well, but I guess there's no telling who it affects."

"Everybody but you," I commented.

"I've had my moments, but you have to understand, I'm a woman. I've given birth to three children, so I'm more than used to living through a little pain."

Mr. Odogo looked up and saw us watching him. He gestured for us to come closer.

"You have seen that there are problems," he said.

"How bad do they have it?" I asked.

"Very, very bad."

"So they're not going to summit?"

"No, no. They must be taken down the mountain immediately. Two of them need to be carried down."

"Carried...by who?" I asked.

"The porters."

"But they're both *huge*."

"It will take all the porters, plus the cook and me, to bring them down."

"And the rest of us?" Doris asked.

"You must wait here."

"For how long?" I asked.

"We shall come back as soon as possible. By this coming afternoon at the latest. Sarah will stay with you to watch and cook. I will come back to bring you down the mountain as soon as possible."

"You mean down the mountain after we've reached the summit?" Sarah asked.

He shook his head. "I do not think so."

"But why couldn't we just summit when you come back?" she demanded.

"There will not be enough food or porters to support your climb. I cannot put you and the others at risk. Perhaps another time."

I should have felt bitter disappointment; instead, I only felt the bitter cold and a sense of relief. I didn't have to go up the mountain and it wasn't my fault. I had a way out. I was saved and—

"But we have to go!" Sarah snapped. She turned to me, I guess looking for support. I didn't answer.

"We have to go up, right?" she said, even more emphatically.

I slowly shook my head. "I think we have to listen to your father."

Sarah did a double take, and even in the dim light I could see her eyes firing daggers into me.

"But your grandfather, the promise you made to him." She turned to her father. "The promise you made to your father that you would get DJ to the top? What of that promise?"

"Life and death are more important. I must get these men to the bottom or they might die. Will their death lessen the death of this boy's grandfather?"

Doris slipped an arm around Sarah. "He's right, dear. There's no choice. Sometimes it just doesn't work out. There'll be other times for you."

But not for Doris, and probably not for me. What if somebody else brought up the ashes, wouldn't that be almost as good? It was the delivery and not the messenger that mattered. Besides he'd written in that last letter that it was the trying that mattered. When had I ever believed *that*? Not until now.

Sarah looked like she agreed and understood, which I'd learned didn't mean anything. "I need to get to the summit," she said.

"You will have to put your needs aside," her father said.

"It is not just my needs, but all of the women and girls who—"

"Enough!" he snapped, cutting her off. "This is not about you, and there will be no further discussion. There is more than your wounded pride at stake. There are lives in the balance, and I do not have the time to debate this now."

That was enough to shut her up—the first time I had seen that happen.

"Do you understand?" he asked.

"Yes, Father."

"You will stay with these two and care for them. Understood?"

"Yes, Father."

"Do I have your word of honor?"

"I will not leave their sides until you return," she said.

"Good, because—"

One of the porters yelled something, and Mr. Odogo turned toward him and then back to us. "It is time. I will return by late in the afternoon."

"Do you want me to bring them partway down the—"

"I want you to be right here when I return. No higher, no lower."

"Yes, Father."

He turned to leave, then stopped, turned around and gave his daughter a hug. "You are a good girl, Mambiri, like your mother in so many ways, which is why I love you both so much."

With her still in his arms he looked at me.

"And you. You are a good boy...a good young man. Your grandfather must have been proud of you. Must *still* be proud of you."

I didn't know what to say, and before I could even choke out an answer, he was gone. He joined the others, and they started away. Each stretcher was carried by four men while Mr. Odogo supported the third climber. How strange they looked, each wearing a headlamp, the little beams of light leading the way. Within a few dozen steps the men beneath the lights vanished, leaving only the beams visible, bobbing down the slope in two little clusters.

I turned off my headlamp, and we were temporarily thrown into darkness before our eyes adjusted to the light of the stars and full moon. Everything was brightly lit. I could see the whole campsite, not just our tents, but those of the other parties, all waiting to start the summit. The tents were blowing in the wind, bobbing about as if they were either trying to escape down the mountain or rise up to meet the cliffs above us, wanting to reach the top. It looked like the fingers of snow at the top were almost glowing, reflecting the bright light of the full moon. Now that I didn't have to climb it, it seemed beautiful.

"Thanks a lot for supporting me," Sarah said.

"I'm not here to support you," I said. "The porters are here to support us."

"Let's not fight," Doris said. "I know this is a disappointment for everybody."

Everybody but me, I thought. This was the answer to my prayers. This was a way out without going up, without being a failure for not being able to make it.

"We'll just stick together and wait it out," Doris said.

Sarah mumbled something under her breath in her own language, but I understood how angry and disappointed she was. I turned away and walked to the edge of the camp. All around us at the other camps I could hear people being woken up, coming to life, getting ready for the climb. I wondered how many of them would make it, how many of them would have liked an *honorable* way not to have to climb.

I pulled out my phone. It had a signal. I could contact my mother…let her know…I better let her know. No, I thought, not my mother, I'd contact my brother. I scrolled through to his name and started typing in my message.

It's over. I couldn't do it. Things happened.

I should have said more, but I didn't really know what more to say. I pushed *Send* and it was gone. I needed to get back to sleep, or at least lie down. He'd probably get it tomorrow and—my phone pinged.

W@ u mean couldn't do it? Break your neck?

I needed to give him more.

Three of the people in our party got acute mountain sickness and had to be taken down the mountain. All the guides and porters except one had to go down.

I sent the message. I wondered how he'd reply. Another ping.

How close r u 2 top?

Did that mean distance or time or effort? They were all so different.

Thirteen hundred meters. Six hours. I can see it, but I was told by the guide not to go, that I couldn't go up.

Within seconds I received his reply.

If u can c it, u can do it. Just go to the top.

That was so much like Steve. Flaunting the rules, just doing what he wanted to do, not listening.

My phone pinged once more.

Just because someone says you can't do something doesn't mean you can't. Grandfather was exhausted and terrified. His friends were being killed all around him, but he kept going because he believed in something. It was a long time ago and that something failed, but he kept going as long as he could.

I choked back a sob. He didn't understand. It wasn't just that I was being told what to do… I couldn't do it. Why didn't he understand that? Maybe because I hadn't told him.

I'm tired. I'm sick. I don't think I can do it. I'm so sorry.

My finger hesitated over the *Send* button. Could I really tell him that? I'd always had to be the strong one. I didn't feel so strong. I pushed *Send.* Almost instantly I felt better and worse, relieved and worried.

The phone pinged again.

Don't be sorry. Go through the tired. Go through the pain. Believe you can do it. Try and you can't fail. You're as good as Grandfather. I believe in you. KUTGW bro. Grandfather's waiting at the top. KIT.

"And I believe in you," I said. One more message to send.

`I'll try little`—I backspaced out the last word. `I'll try, for Grandpa and for you, bro. T4BU.`

I sent the message and put away the phone. I walked over to where Doris and Sarah stood, watching the little dots of light making their way up the mountain.

"It's mesmerizing," Doris said.

"Beautiful," Sarah added. "It's just so sad that—"

"I'm going to climb it," I said.

They both looked at me in shock.

"I'm not asking either of you to go with me," I said. "But I have to try."

"I'm going with you," Doris said.

"And neither of you are going," Sarah said. "At least not without me."

"You don't have to come with us," I said. "We'll just follow the lights of other people and use their guides."

"Besides, we don't want you to break your promise to your father," Doris added.

"That is why I *must* go with you, to keep my promise," she said.

"How do you think that climbing with us will do that?" I questioned.

"I promised him I'd stay right with you. If you two leave and I remain here, I am breaking my promise. Besides, he cannot stop us; we will be up and back down, waiting for him when he arrives."

"So you're not going to tell him we did it?" I asked.

"Oh, no, I will tell him."

"And he won't be mad?"

"Oh, he will be *very* mad, but I will accept my punishment. Sometimes you simply must act and then take the punishment. Besides, being disobedient is one thing, but being a liar is another. I am often disobedient, but I am never dishonest."

"I guess that might mean something when it comes time for him to punish you," I said.

She shrugged. "No matter what he says or does, it will not take away what I have done. I, a Chagga woman, will have stood on the roof of Africa."

The roof of Africa. That sounded almost magical. No, more than magical, almost *mythical.*

"Let us put on our clothing, gather water, strap on our packs and begin," Sarah said.

TWENTY-TWO

Sarah led, Doris tucked in right behind her, and I was at the end, where I could reach up and support Doris if she slipped. There was nobody to support me if I fell backward, but it was better if they were in front of me—*uphill* of me. It wasn't like either of them—or the two of them together—could do anything more than cushion me. If I fell from the top of the line, I'd simply knock the three of us over.

The path was narrow and steep with many hairpin turns across the face of the slope. Sarah was in charge of finding the cutbacks, discovering the best footholds as we climbed. Every time the path became more vertical, I felt it in my chest and lungs and I just wanted a flatter section to cross the face. Every time we hit one of those flatter spots, I thought how we needed to climb more steeply. We had 1,200 meters to gain, and the only way to do that was to go up.

While Sarah was leading us, we were merely a small part of a wave of lights going up the slope. All the climbers on the seven different trails came together on this section, the only way to the summit. Little groups of lights, three or four or five people to a group, flickered ahead of us or behind us. Each time we stopped, we were passed by a group of climbers, and as we continued to climb, we would pass others who had slumped over to rest. It felt good to pass anybody, although it was more like a game of leap-frog; those we passed would pass us at our next rest, and those who had gone before us would be reeled back in as they rested and we continued.

Often a few words of encouragement would be passed back and forth, sometimes in languages I couldn't understand, but the smiles, thumbs-up and pats on the back were universal. We were all in this together, traveling separately, not knowing each other's names, but going to the same place. Well, at least we hoped we were going to the same place. With some, I wasn't so certain.

We'd passed more than one group where a member was hunched over, throwing up. Others were sobbing. Some were simply staring into space, their expressions blank and hopeless. Their bodies were still on the hill, but their minds were elsewhere. I knew how all of them felt. My stomach was moving more quickly than my feet, and my head continued to throb, the pain moving from the back to the sides to the front. I couldn't help but wonder what would come first, the end of the climb or the end of my ability to climb.

"I need to stop," Doris gasped.

"Just up ahead is a place to sit," Sarah said. "Can you make it?"

"Yes...yes."

Our already slow pace slowed down even more. Little steps became baby steps as I focused on Doris in front of me. Her stride—which I matched—was so small that the back of one step was barely in front of the toe of the other.

"Right here," Sarah said.

We slumped down onto some rocks at a place where the path had widened slightly. I pulled off my pack and helped Doris with hers.

"I'm so sorry for slowing us down," Doris said.

"You're not slowing anybody down," I replied. "I was just getting ready to ask if we could stop."

"You are a very sweet liar."

"I'm not lying. Well, not much. You asked to break just before I was going to. This is hard."

"Very hard," Sarah said. "Very hard. Everyone must take water."

I pulled off my gloves and fumbled with my stiff fingers to pull out my insulated water bottle. Without the insulation, the water would have frozen. Unscrewing the top, I poured the cold water into my parched mouth. It felt good, tracing a line down to my upset stomach.

"How far have we gone?" Doris asked.

I looked at my watch. It glowed under my headlamp. "It's just after two, so we've been climbing for almost two hours."

"But how *far* have we gone?" she asked.

We both looked at Sarah. She shook her head. "I do not know. Maybe a third...maybe a quarter of the way. Remember, I have never climbed this mountain before either."

As we sat there, another group shuffled up the path. Sarah said something to the guide in the lead, and he responded. They exchanged another burst of words and then she got to her feet.

"He said that we are almost one third of the way," she said. "And he said he hopes I make it."

"That was very sweet of him," Doris said.

Sweet and reassuring and disturbing all at once. Could I go twice the distance I'd already gone? Could Doris?

"He also said that the mountain is not coming to us. He said I should get you up and start forward."

Slowly I got to my feet and then offered Doris a hand, which she took, and I pulled her up.

"One step at a time," I said to her. "And we'll stop and smell any flowers that we find."

She laughed. "Promises, promises."

Sarah started up the path, Doris behind and me tight behind her. One step at a time, each step one closer to the top and one farther from the bottom.

We'd fallen into a pattern. We'd move upward for somewhere between ten and fifteen minutes and then stop, drink some water, catch our breath, let our hearts settle and then start up again. We leaned against the rock face but never sat down. Standing back up was too hard. The cold was getting worse. It seemed to insinuate itself between the layers of clothing, and my toes and fingertips were numb and tingly. I would have complained if I hadn't noticed that Sarah didn't have gloves. She tucked her hands into the pockets of a coat that wasn't nearly as warm as the one I was wearing over top layers of clothing. I suspected she didn't have as many layers. If this was cold for me, it had to be frigid for her. She didn't complain. Which meant I couldn't complain. I wanted to complain. I wanted to stop moving forward. I wanted to curl up into a little ball and be carried back down to my tent. No—back to my bed in my house.

At least I didn't feel like throwing up anymore. My stomach had finally realized that there was no point in trying to eject something that wasn't there. Instead, all the blood seemed to be rushing to my head. I could feel it circulating, moving from lobe to lobe. There was so much pressure on my brain that I would occasionally reach up to touch my head, to confirm that it wasn't actually physically bigger.

"Would it be all right if we stopped again?" Doris asked.

She slumped slightly backward as she spoke, and I lifted up my hands and placed them against her back to give her a little bit of a cushion. We shuffled forward another two dozen steps—baby steps—until Sarah found a spot suitable for stopping. Instantly I slumped against a rock, half leaning, half sitting. Sarah remained standing, but Doris was on the ground! I got back to my feet and shuffled over to her.

"Are you all right?"

"Just lost my balance a little. Luckily I'm so short, the ground wasn't far away." She gave a weak little smile.

"Water, take some water," I said. I pulled out my thermos.

"That's your water," she replied. "You'll need all of it to get to the top."

"It's *our* water and we'll need it to get *all* of us to the top."

She didn't answer.

I undid the top of the thermos and handed it to her. "Doris, I wouldn't be here without you. I wouldn't have made it this far. We're doing this together." I never thought I'd say these words, let alone mean them, but they were true. We were in this together.

"I just don't think I can," she whispered.

"I don't know if I can either, but either we head up together or we head back down together."

"You can't do that!" she protested. "What about your grandfather?"

"My grandpa wouldn't have left you behind."

"I'm just slowing you down."

"We'll go at whatever pace we need to go. We're a team. We aren't slowing each other down, we're moving each other forward. Together. When you're ready, we'll start to move again."

She smiled. "I'm ready."

"Well, I'm not," I said. "I need some water... and so do you."

She took a big swig from the bottle and then handed it to me.

"How's your head?" she asked.

"It could be worse." That wasn't a lie. It could have exploded.

I took a second pull from my bottle and then did something I was trying to avoid. I looked up. I could see a few lights bobbing up the slope above us—well above us—and then…nothing. I knew better than to think that was the top. It was just another place where the slope changed angles, preventing us from seeing farther. Then I looked below. There were more lights—two more parties visible—still below us, still moving up. We still had people below pushing us forward and people above pulling us up. We weren't alone, not when the three of us were together. I remembered Grandpa's words from the letter: *If you want to travel far, travel together.*

"We must go," Sarah said.

I offered Doris a hand, and for a brief second I thought her weight was going to tumble me over. How weak was I? I slipped the thermos into the opening on the side of my bag and pulled my gloves back on.

There was a nightmare quality to our climb now. The exhaustion, the sleep deprivation, the cold, the strange shuffling of strangers with lights on their heads. It was a zombie movie. Zombies climbing a mountain, and I was one of the zombies.

Sarah turned around. "Turn off your lights."

"What?"

"Your lights. Turn them off."

With numb, gloved fingers I reached up and attempted to push the switch to turn it off. Doris turned off her light and then I managed to turn mine off too. It was darker, but not dark. In fact, as my eyes adjusted, it was almost bright. The whole scene was bathed in a soft white light. Rather than seeing less, we could see more. Not limited by the bright little pool of light directly in front of us, we could see even into the distance and up the slope.

"The moon is so bright," Doris said.

I looked around until I could locate it. It was bright...but that bright?

"Not just the moon. The sun is starting to glow over the horizon," Sarah said.

"What time is it?" I asked.

"Almost five, I believe," she said.

I looked at my watch—something I'd been avoiding—turning it so that the dial received enough light. It was a quarter to five.

"We've been climbing for almost five hours," Doris said. "Well...climbing and resting."

"You cannot do the first without the second," Sarah said. "To climb straight would be almost impossible."

"Completely impossible, at least for us," I said. "You'd have to be Chagga to do that."

"Most Chagga could not," Sarah said. "We are doing well."

"How much longer do we have to keep doing well?" I asked.

"Look up. You see where the top disappears, just beyond those climbers?"

"That's the top?"

"Not the top. Stella's Point. Beyond that no more than an hour."

Reassured and crushed at the same time.

"We must move again. The hill will not come to us."

I nodded my head. I pushed myself up and to my feet and tumbled over! I was wearing so many clothes and so much of my body was numb, that there was no pain. I felt embarrassed and confused more than anything. I struggled to get back to my feet and again I collapsed, my legs not able to support me.

"Just stay down," Sarah said.

"I have to get—"

"Just for a few seconds. Just rest lying down."

"Do what she says," Doris added. "There's no energy left for arguing."

She was right. I had no energy, not to argue, not to talk, and certainly not to get up.

Sarah reached underneath me. Was she trying to lift me? She snapped the clips on my pack and pulled it off me.

"What are you doing?" I gasped.

"Lightening your load. Now let us help you roll over."

Together, Doris and Sarah took my hands and helped spin me around so I was in a sitting position.

"Now take some water," Sarah said. Doris handed me the water bottle.

I took a long sip. As the water settled in, I could almost feel the energy returning. At least enough to get to my feet, I hoped.

"I'm ready." I stood up. Shaky but working. "Let me put on my pack and—"

"I am carrying your pack," Sarah said.

"I can take it."

"You must listen to your guide. I will give it back to you at Stella's Point."

"No arguing," Doris said. "Didn't you offer to take my bag when I wasn't able?"

"Of course." I paused. "I just thought that... that—"

"That you'd be the one carrying somebody else's extra bag? Perhaps that of an old woman?" Doris asked.

"Perhaps an *older* woman," I said.

"You've been carrying a lot of weight around on those shoulders," she said. "It's a sign of strength to know when you need help. We're all here to help each other."

I brushed away a tear. "I don't know what to say."

"You don't have to say anything. We're a team, remember? Just climb. All the way to the top."

"All the way to the top," I said.

TWENTY-THREE

I heard noise coming from above and looked past Doris and Sarah. It was hikers coming down the mountain. Had they given up this close to the top? No, that wasn't it. They had reached the summit and were coming back down!

I'd seen the three men and two women before at the base camp and on one of the other days' hikes. They were all in their twenties and fit.

"It's not much farther!" one of them yelled out. He had a strong Australian accent.

"You're doing great!" one of the women said.

"What's it like?" Doris asked.

The woman smiled. "You're going to find out for yourself soon enough."

One of the men moved in close, wrapping an arm around me and putting his mouth right by my ear. "What you're doing for your grand-mum is pretty special, mate."

I needed to correct him about one of those things. "What she's doing for me is even more special."

He slapped me on the back. "No more talking. Get climbing."

The hikers slipped past us and down the slope, kicking up a cloud of volcanic dust as they braced themselves, fighting gravity in a different way.

"Sarah," I called out. "Can I have my pack...please."

She didn't answer.

"I need to carry Grandpa. I have to keep my word."

She hesitated.

"I'm all right. I can do it."

She took the pack off her back and handed it to me. I put it on. Strangely the added weight seemed to make me feel lighter.

Sarah turned up the slope and began shuffling forward. We fell into line behind her.

It was becoming lighter. The sun was still not up, but the rays were bouncing above the horizon. I could almost feel them and the warmth that they were bringing. It gave me renewed energy.

With the light came the opportunity to see farther. The slope had become wider, opening up so there seemed to be multiple paths rather than one path. Turning back, I saw there were other hikers lower down, still struggling over the parts that we'd completed. I wanted to yell back encouragement to them. They were strangers, but we were all in this together.

There was no longer solid rock underneath our feet. There was loose ash, shifting down as we pushed up, and loose rocks, some rolling back as I pushed against them to gain my footing. Another party—two women—slid down the hill off to the side on another path. Another group had made it. It didn't matter that they'd gotten there first. It just mattered that we were going to get there. I was almost certain.

"Stop here," Sarah said.

I almost bumped into Doris. I felt like I could go farther and I didn't want to stop. Then I saw the sign: *Welcome to Stella's Point!* We were almost there. My mind raced back to what I could remember.

The slope was supposed to flatten out now. There was less than 200 meters left to climb.

Doris took out her camera. "I want a picture of you two here before we go on."

Sarah and I bookended the sign, and Doris snapped a picture.

"Now you," I said.

I took the camera as she took my place. I slipped off my glove and realized that my fingers felt fine. The chill was gone from them. I looked up. I was going to say "smile," but both of them already were. I snapped the picture and then took a second, just in case.

As we stood there, two more parties came by on their way down. They were smiling and laughing and every single person offered us encouragement, cheering us on. And each word just gave me a little more energy, a little more incentive, a little more inspiration. Without saying another word, we started up again.

We pushed up the slope, reaching the crest. I looked beyond Sarah, over her head. As we climbed one side, the sun rose over the other. It was blindingly bright. I shielded my eyes with a gloved hand until they adjusted. I looked out in front of us. The ground flattened until it was barely rising. And there, no more than 200 meters away, was a small group of people crowded around a sign post—*the* sign post.

"Is it?" I asked.

"We are here," Sarah said. Her voice was filled with wonderment.

"Almost there," I said. "Still a few more steps to go."

"One step at a time," Doris said. "DJ, you should go ahead."

"What?"

"You go ahead. You and your grandfather."

"No. You, Sarah, me and my grandpa. Together."

I reached out and took her hand and then Sarah's. "All the way to the top. Together."

Three astride, we walked up the little slope. The rush of adrenaline pushed aside the tiredness in my legs, the strain in my lungs, the pain in my head. For the first time in days I was certain we were going to make it.

"I wish my husband could see me now," Doris said.

"He can," I said. "The same way my grandpa can see me."

As we reached the sign, the crowd parted. They offered smiles, and a man—a stranger on the same journey—shook my hand and offered congratulations.

"Let me take your picture," he said.

Doris gave him her camera, and the three of us climbed in front of the sign and stood there. *Uhuru Point—the Highest Point in Africa.* All the way to the top. I felt like laughing. I felt like crying. I just felt...so alive.

TWENTY-FOUR

I stood off to the side, clutching the cane. I'd done what I'd been asked. I was at the top of Mount Kilimanjaro. I could sprinkle the ashes and then go down, go home. It would be over. Now that I was here, I didn't want it to be over. Until the ashes were sprinkled, it was like he was still with me. But that was wrong. He'd *always* be with me.

"We need to get going," Sarah said. "Soon."

I nodded. "I understand. Just another minute."

"We understand, dear," Doris said. "Do you want to be alone?"

"No. I want you here. I'm just trying to figure out what to say. I should say something."

"Would you mind if I said a few words?" she asked.

"No, of course not."

Sarah and Doris removed their hats and I pulled off my balaclava. In my one hand was the cane, and in the other my grandpa's beret.

"We are here to say goodbye to David McLean," Doris said. "I did not have the good fortune to know the man, but I have been blessed to know his grandson. David, they say that you can tell a tree by the fruit. I have known the fruit. To produce such a fine grandson, you must have been a fine man. You are missed."

I felt myself choking up, trying to fight back the tears, and then I heard sobbing. I turned. It was Sarah and she was crying, her whole body convulsing.

"You asked a favor of your grandson, a favor we will now complete. I have a favor of you. Could you say hello to my husband, and make sure he isn't causing too much trouble up there?"

I unscrewed the top of the cane and slowly dumped the ashes into the palm of my hand.

The wind, which had been strong, seemed to pause, waiting.

"Thanks for taking *me* along on this trip," I said to Grandpa.

I tossed the ashes into the air. The wind picked them up and they flew up in an iridescent white cloud and then were grabbed and lifted higher and higher until I couldn't see them anymore, until they were someplace between heaven and earth.

"It's not goodbye," I said softly. "You'll always be with me."

TWENTY-FIVE

My eyes popped open, and in the pitch black my hand went up to my head to push on my headlamp. It wasn't there. And then I realized that *I* wasn't there...on the mountain. I was in a bed in a room at the Springlands Hotel in Moshi. I let out a big sigh of relief and satisfaction. I'd gotten to the top and back down to the bottom. I closed my eyes again. The bed felt good.

In the morning I'd be flying out. From Moshi to Nairobi to Amsterdam to home. It would be a long journey, and I needed to get back to sleep, but I couldn't help thinking about the day ahead. I'd get dressed, finish packing, take my grandpa's cane and meet Doris, Sarah and Mr. Odogo in the lobby. They were going to be driving us to the airport. I'd be sharing the first flight with Doris and then we'd go our separate ways.

I wasn't looking forward to saying goodbye to her, but it wasn't going to be a forever goodbye. We'd promised to get together next summer. It wasn't the usual "see you sometime" arrangement. We'd agreed that I'd fly over to England and she'd show me around. She even threatened me with a granddaughter she wanted me to meet. If she was anything like her grandmother, it wasn't a threat. Maybe she'd even have two granddaughters worth meeting. I'd already asked Steve to join me, and he'd said yes. It would be a great trip for us to share.

I really missed him. I didn't know if that would last once we were together again, but who knew? He was my brother, and more than that, my twin brother. I was sure that within a couple of weeks we'd start to drive each other crazy again, but still, wasn't that what brothers did? And probably what brothers and sisters did too.

That's what Sarah had become—my sister. Despite all the kidding around, she'd never be my girlfriend or my wife, but she would always be my little sister. My annoying, irritating, bossy, opinionated little sister who I cared for very much—even if I never saw her again. Maybe I could help her realize her dreams the way my grandpa had helped her grandpa. I'd already been part of one dream, although she probably didn't need much help from anybody to achieve the others. Maybe she'd remember me kindly when she became the first female president of Tanzania.

I was going to miss Mr. Odogo as well. A few days ago I wouldn't have believed that was possible.

We had arrived back at the base camp from the summit about an hour before Mr. Odogo arrived. As soon as he got there, Sarah told him what we had done. I'd held my breath, waiting for the explosion. How he reacted wasn't what I had expected. He offered us each congratulations, a handshake and a hug. He said that he was "too proud to be angry" with us. In fact, he said that he had expected us to climb, that he knew his daughter too well, and knew that I was going to keep my promise to my grandpa. It seemed that he had faith in me even when I didn't.

That didn't stop him from punishing us though. Instead of allowing us to stay and rest at the base camp, he marched us partway down the mountain. After ten hours and 1,300 meters up to the summit and back down to base camp, the last thing I needed was to move again. He pushed us another 10 kilometers, down another 1,400 meters. Sarah had told me that if Doris hadn't been with us he would have marched us all the way off the mountain, shedding another 1,500 meters over another 8 kilometers. Thank goodness for Doris. Not just for up there on the mountain but for down here at the hotel...and in the future.

I sat up in bed—my nice comfortable bed. It was becoming clearer as my mind came alive that I wasn't going to be able to go back to sleep. Maybe it was almost time to get up. I sat up, turned on the light and reached for my phone. It was almost five—too early to get up but too late to go back to sleep. And then I noticed I had emails and texts. That wasn't surprising.

Since I'd gotten down from the mountain, I'd been exchanging messages with all my cousins. Up there, pushed to the limit, it had been easy to forget that I wasn't the only one on an adventure. I didn't know where Rennie was, but the rest of us were scattered around the world—Steve in Spain; Adam in France; and Spencer, Bernard and Webb in North America. In those brief messages I'd gotten little snippets of their adventures.

I couldn't wait to sit down and tell them about my journey, but more important, hear all about their quests. I could picture us all sitting around at the cottage with our parents, sharing our stories with each other. But there would always be one person missing. The person who launched us on our trips and gave us so much, the person who would have enjoyed the stories more than anybody. But really, he wouldn't be missing. He'd been right there beside me the whole way up the mountain and he'd still be with me—with us—when we gathered again.

Then I remembered. I still had one more part of Grandpa with me right now. The last letter still to be read. It was buried somewhere in my pack.

I climbed out of bed and pulled things out that I'd already packed. I started to feel a little panicky—where was it?—and then I found it. It was bent out of shape, a bit worse for wear.

I'd originally thought that I should read it at the top of the mountain, but in the excitement it had slipped my mind. Coming back down, I did remember but I wondered if the word on the front—*End*—really meant the bottom of the mountain. Then when I got to the bottom, I thought maybe it meant when I got home or...Really, I guess part of me just didn't want to open it. It was the last thing he was ever going to say to me.

I held the letter in my hands, turning it over slowly. I thought about what had happened over the past weeks and I thought about him, what he had meant to me, what he *still* meant to me. It was time to open the letter. I unsealed it, careful not to rip the envelope, and pulled out the letter.

Dear DJ,

With the first two letters I knew where you would most likely be when you opened them; probably in your bedroom for the first, and at the foot of the mountain for the second. This one, well, it's hard to say what "end" means. It might mean you reached the top of Kilimanjaro or it might mean that you couldn't. It doesn't matter. To be honest with you, it never mattered. What truly matters is not the path that lies behind you or before you—what matters is what is inside of you.

You are such a strong, capable person. Somebody who always seems to succeed in the tasks he has set. I hope this gift that you gave to me—taking me up the mountain—was also a gift to you. I hope you have learned the joy of taking life as it comes, living in the moment, not thinking through to the end, but relishing the process and perhaps going polepole—going slowly along the path you travel.

You'll have to excuse me for my feeble attempts to communicate wisdom. I was always amazed when people saw me as wise. It seems to be a by-product of growing old; if you are old, you must be wise. Believe me, I've met a whole lot of stupid old people, most of whom were positive they were wise. Wisdom is almost an illusion.

A fool believes he knows what life is about. A wiser man understands he knows little. The wisest man not only understands his limitations, but accepts and embraces that lack of understanding. Slowly, over the years, I came to appreciate that what I knew would never be as great as what I didn't know. The only thing I have come to know with certainty is that all of us are simply trying to get along the best that we can, sharing in our struggles, *trying for our dreams, living with our failures and celebrating our successes. I've had my share of both.*

With you, I've often wondered if your greatest disadvantage was that you're so used to succeeding. Failure is good for the soul. While we aim for success, it is the failure that defines us. Don't be afraid of failing. You need to accept it and understand that failing doesn't make you a failure. It merely makes you human. I hope through this trip you have learned a few things, but the most important is that life is a journey, not a destination. This was part of your life journey—the last part I will share with you—although I know that a part of me will always be with you.

The Chagga people believe that a man never dies as long as he has children. I believe that as well. Through my daughters, through my grandsons, I live on. Through you I live on. I am so proud of you and sad that I will not be there to watch your ongoing journey to manhood, to becoming a husband and father and grandfather. And through your children and their children I will live on. Part of me will always be here on earth. The rest—I guess that's something I now know but can't pass on to you.

There is still one more thing I'd like to ask of you—and no, it doesn't involve climbing any more mountains! Having you named after me was such an honor. Your mother gave me one of the most precious things in a life that was filled with so much. Of course two Davids in a family led to you being called David Junior and then DJ. Now there's no longer a senior, so there's no longer a junior. You could—and only if you wish—now be known as David, but only if you wanted, and only someday if it feels right to you. And who knows? There might, many, many years from now, be born a son or grandson who would be named David to carry on both of our legacies. If that does happen, I want you to do two things: give him our beret. And don't make him climb any damn mountains!

Socrates was once asked to comment on whether or not a man had led a good life. He said he could not say until the man had died because his life was not over. I can now answer. I've had the best life imaginable. And it ended, not back where I died but up on that mountain. Thank you for taking me with you on this trip—thanks to you, I finally have been between heaven and earth.

With greatest love,

Grandpa

I fought unsuccessfully to hold back the tears. But I knew these tears weren't just about sadness. Mixed in were gratitude, relief, happiness and joy.

There on the bed, among the items I'd unpacked to get to the letter, was the beret. It had been buried in my pack. I picked it up, felt the material, turned it around in my hands and thought of him wearing it, a smile on his face, a spring in his step, telling stories, laughing and living and loving each moment of his life.

I put it on, but somehow it just didn't feel right. I walked over to the mirror and rearranged it, turning it a little this way, pulling it down slightly, until it looked right. Then I looked into the mirror. And I saw him looking back at me. We were both smiling.

ACKNOWLEDGMENTS

Many thanks to the other wonderful writers of this series—what an honor it was to share the process with you all! Thanks also to Andrew Wooldridge for taking a chance on the series and actually getting back from lunch, and to Sarah Harvey for editing seven stories by seven very different writers.

ERIC WALTERS began writing in 1993 as a way to entice his grade-five students into becoming more interested in reading and writing. Since then, Eric has published over seventy novels and won over eighty awards. Often his stories incorporate themes that reflect his background in education and social work and his commitment to humanitarian and social-justice issues. Eric lives in Mississauga, Ontario, with his wife and three children. For more information, visit www.ericwalters.net.

Eric, his son Nick and Nick's friend Jack climbed Mount Kilimanjaro to research this book.

Eric founded and helps operate a children's program that provides for over 400 orphans in Kikima, Mbooni District, Kenya. For more information, and to find out how you can help, go to www.creationofhope.com.

THE SEVEN SERIES

7 GRANDSONS
7 JOURNEYS
7 AUTHORS
1 AMAZING SERIES

ERIC WALTERS
BETWEEN HEAVEN AND EARTH
9781554699414

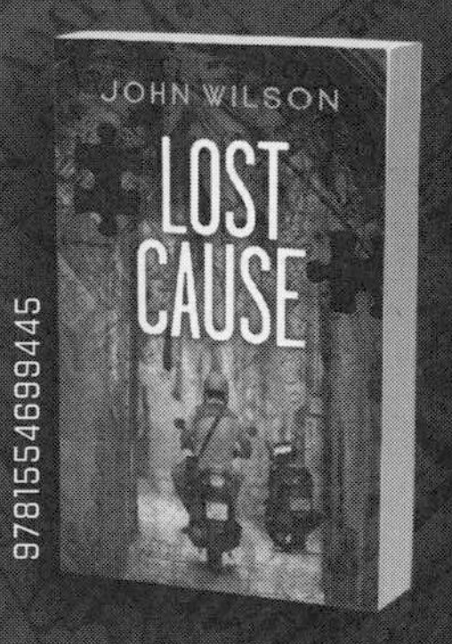
JOHN WILSON
LOST CAUSE
9781554699445

TED STAUNTON
JUMP CUT
9781554699476

RICHARD SCRIMGER
INK ME
9781459800168

CLOSE TO THE HEEL
9781554699506

SIGMUND BROUWER
DEVIL'S PASS
9781554699384

SHANE PEACOCK
LAST MESSAGE
9781554699353

SEVEN THE SERIES
BETWEEN HEAVEN AND EARTH WALTERS
LOST CAUSE WILSON
JUMP CUT STAUNTON
INK ME SCRIMGER
CLOSE TO THE HEEL McCLINTOCK
DEVIL'S PASS BROUWER
LAST MESSAGE PEACOCK
SHANE PEACOCK
LAST MESSAGE
9781459802704